QUILT BLOCK

A Quilters Club Mystery

"Pink Dogwoods in Appliqué,"
the 1925 quilt by Marie D. Webster.

QUILT BLOCK

A Quilters Club Mystery

Marjory Sorrell Rockwell

ABSOLUTELY AMAZING eBOOKS

"In the crazy quilt of life, I'm glad you're in my block of friends."

-anon.

Quilters Club Mysteries

By Marjory Sorrell Rockwell

A Christmas Quit (Prequel)
The Quilters Club Quartet
The Quilters Club Trio
The Underhanded Stitch
The Patchwork Puzzler
Coming Unraveled
Hemmed In
Sewed Up Tight
All Tangled Up
Needled
Stitch In Time
Cross Stitch
Fat Quarters
Stitch in the Ditch

**Available from
AbsolutelyAmazingEbooks.com**

QUILT BLOCK

A Quilters Club Mystery

TABLE OF CONTENTS

Chapter One
Sharks in the Sky

Chapter Two
Meet Robert De Niro

Chapter Three
Marie Daugherty Webster

Chapter Four
Catch and ...

Chapter Five
A Murder to Investigate

Chapter Six
Lawyering Up

Chapter Seven
... Release

Chapter Eight
The Bad Movie

Chapter Nine
What About Martin?

Chapter Ten
On the Case

Chapter Eleven
Back to School

Chapter Twelve
Chilly Willy

Chapter Thirteen
On the Ground News

Chapter Fourteen
The Tornado

Chapter Fifteen
Damage Report

Chapter Sixteen
Eyewitness Accounts

Chapter Seventeen
Crimestopper Tip

Chapter Eighteen
Coming Out

Chapter Nineteen
History of Twisters

Chapter Twenty
Help Arrives

Chapter Twenty-One
No Second Sight

Chapter Twenty-Two
Side Trips

Chapter Twenty-Three
Gimme Shelter

Chapter Twenty-Four
View from the Top

Chapter Twenty-Five
Sign Off

Chapter Twenty-Six
Philanthropical Activities

Chapter Twenty-Seven
Searching

Chapter Twenty-Eight
Open for Business

Chapter Twenty-Nine
Helen of Troy

Chapter Thirty
Margie's List

Chapter Thirty-One
Living in a Castle

Chapter Thirty-Two
The Old History Teacher

Chapter Thirty-Three
Septuagenarian Stalker

Chapter Thirty-Four
The Scoop

Chapter Thirty-Five
N'yen's Brainstorm

Chapter Thirty-Six
Maddy's Distraction

Chapter Thirty-Seven
With a Lead Pipe

Chapter Thirty-Eight
Time to Leave

Chapter Thirty-Nine
The Sister

Chapter Forty
An Irreplaceable Artifact

Chapter Forty-One
A New Home

Chapter Forty-Two
Getting a Bodyguard

Chapter Forty-Three
Danger, Danger

Chapter Forty-Four
Prodigal Daughter

Chapter Forty-Five
Gun Play

Chapter Forty-Six
The Quilt Is Found

Epilogue

Cast of Characters

End Notes

About the Author

PART I

Suddenly Uncle Henry stood up.

"There's a cyclone coming, Em," he called to his wife. "I'll go look after the stock." Then he ran toward the sheds where the cows and horses were kept.

Aunt Em dropped her work and came to the door. One glance told her of the danger close at hand.

"Quick, Dorothy!" she screamed. "Run for the cellar!"

- L. Frank Baum,
The Wonderful Wizard of Oz

CHAPTER ONE

Sharks in the Sky

Maddy Madison and her granddaughter Aggie were watching a stupid TV movie, *Sharknado: Feeding Frenzy* – a B-grade disaster film about a freak cyclone that scoops man-eating sharks out of the water and rains them down on hapless civilians.

Chomp, chomp, chomp!

"That was silly, Grammy," Aggie rolled her eyes as the movie's end credits scrolled down the screen of the 55-inch TCL 4K Ultra HD TV. The story had ended with the hero and a designated damsel in distress taking shelter in an abandoned shark repellant factory. The idea being they would be safe until the next shark-laden tornado struck – i.e. a future movie sequel. What was this, the seventh or eighth *Sharknado* movie?

"People enjoy silly," replied Maddy. "The ability to laugh at tragedy makes it easier to endure."

"Okay, I can understand that. But the idea of sharks inside a waterspout requires an inordinate suspension of disbelief."

"Ha! You're using a lot of $10 words just to say you found the movie unbelievable," said Beau Madison. Her grandfather had walked into the den looking for popcorn. He could smell the buttery odor from several rooms away. Unfortunately, Maddy and Aggie's oversized bowl was empty except for a few stray kernels.

1

"I'm taking Film Appreciation 101 this semester," she said.

"What happened to just enjoying a movie – without having to get out a scalpel and do an autopsy?" he muttered before heading back into the kitchen to dump some more Orville Redenbacher into the Presto Hot Air Popper. The smell of buttered popcorn had got his taste buds percolating.

"Pay no attention to your grandfather," Maddy patted the girl's hand. "His idea of a good movie is *Rambo*."

"Talk about suspension of disbelief!" giggled Aggie. "That's a cinematic glorification of violence by that troglodyte Sylvester Stallone."

"Oh, don't be so hard on Sly. He did look pretty good beating up that giant Russian in *Rocky IV*."

"Grammy, I think you appreciate his muscles more than his thespian skills."

Beau Madison wandered back into the room. "Let her dream," he counseled his granddaughter. "When you get to be our age, it's one of life's greater pleasures."

"We're going to make a movie this semester at school," announced Aggie. "It's a big project."

"We who?" asked Maddy. The inane shark movie over, she removed her glasses and placed them in a tray on the oak-topped coffee table. She started to pour herself more Diet Pepsi, but discovered the 2-liter plastic bottle was empty.

"My entire class. Our teacher is going to direct. Before he became a film professor, he was a big-time movie director."

"Oh? Have I ever heard of him?" asked her grandmother. She considered herself something of a film buff.

"Martin Lorenzo Griffith. He directed *Three Weddings and a Funeral.*"

"Don't you mean *Four Weddings and a Funeral,* dear?"

"No, this was a prequel. Without Hugh Grant and Andie MacDowell."

"Oh."

"He says we're going to do an adaptation of *The Wizard of Oz* for our project."

"That's nice," said her grandfather before stepping back into the kitchen to check on his popcorn. You could hear the *pop! pop! pippity! pop!* in the background.

"And guess what –?" Aggie called after him. "I've been cast in the lead. Isn't that great?"

"As the Wizard?" asked her grandfather, returning with a heaping bowl of freshly popped corn. You could smell the artificial butter.

"No, as Dorothy. Can't you just see my name in lights? – Agnes Millicent Tidemore!"

"I'm sure you'll be great, dear," Maddy assured her. A pretty fifteen-year-old blonde, Aggie would make a wonderful Dorothy. Maybe her dog Tige could play Toto ... he was a cute little mutt.

"Thanks, Grammy."

But as it happened, the class project got canceled when a few days later Martin Lorenzo Griffith was killed by a man claiming to be Robert De Niro.

~ ~ ~

Maddy Madison belonged to a small sewing circle known as the Quilters Club. The group met every Tuesday in the sewing room at the Hoople Quilting Heritage Museum.

Maddy was the group's unofficial leader. The other members consisted of Lizzie Ridenour, the scrawny-but-glamorous redhead who managed the quilting museum; Cookie Brown, the brainy blonde in charge of the local historical society; and Bootsie Purdue, the pudgy brunette who headed up the sprawling no-kill animal shelter on the edge of town.

Maddy's precocious granddaughter considered herself a member of the Quilters Club too. Lizzie had been tutoring the girl in the fine art of quiltmaking. Aggie's stitches were improving to the point she'd been winning prizes in junior competitions.

While Aggie loved making quilts, she liked solving mysteries even more. And the Quilters Club ladies had earned themselves a minor reputation as amateur detectives. They were the bane of Police Chief Jim Purdue's existence with their unofficial sleuthing. Jim, of course, was Bootsie's husband.

Today, they were making plans for a patchwork quilt that would earn them a place in the Guinness Book of World Records. The project would involve the entire population of Caruthers Corners (all 3,412). They intended to sew the largest quilt in the world – bigger than the recordholder in Portugal. The idea was to have it completed by National Quilting Day in March. That gave them six months, give or take.

Aggie was in school today. She was a sophomore this year. She even had a steady boyfriend, a fellow classmate by the name of Bobby Elwood. Hanging out with him after class, she'd missed several Quilters Club meetings lately. Puberty had kicked in.

Around two o'clock, the gals took a break: Lizzie checked her voice mail. Cookie phoned her assistant at the Historical Society to get a report on today's attendance. Maddy added a few items to her Food Lion shopping list. Bootsie called her husband to see if he would be home for supper on time.

Ten minutes later they reassembled in the sewing room. There was still much planning to do. Their goal was to cover the entire Town Square – 10 acres in all – with a community-made patchwork quilt. Very ambitious, to say the least.

"Hey everybody," interrupted Bootsie. "News Flash: Jim just told me there was a shooting at Caruthers High!" As the police chief's wife, she had an inside pipeline to such info.

"A school shooting?" cried Lizzie. "How many students were killed?"

"Who did it?" Cookie wanted to know. "Some psycho kid? An ISIS terrorist convert?"

"Oh my God!" shrieked Maddy Madison. "Is Aggie safe?" Hands pressed to her cheeks like that kid in *Home Alone*. How could something like that happen here in Caruthers Corners, Indiana?

"No, no, no," Bootsie tried to clarify her words. "No students were injured. Someone shot a teacher."

"Which teacher?" asked Lizzie. Looking for lurid details. She lived on gossip and startling headlines. She just couldn't restrain herself.

"Jim didn't say."

Turned out, it was the one-time director of *Three Weddings and a Funeral*.

CHAPTER TWO

Meet Robert De Niro

"It was horrible!" exclaimed Aggie. "That crazy man barged into my Film Appreciation class and shot the teacher – bang, bang, bang!"

"Three shots?" asked Cookie. Always looking for specific facts.

"Three or maybe four."

"Are you okay?" asked Maddy. Checking her granddaughter for bullet holes.

"Oh, Grammy, I'm fine. But my teacher's dead as a Thanksgiving turkey." The holiday was coming up next month.

"Oh my."

"Mr. Griffith was my favorite teacher," sniffled Aggie. She plopped down in a wingback chair and buried her face in her hands.

Immediately after hearing about the shooting, the Quilters Club had rushed *en masse* over to the girl's house to check on her well-being. The Tidemores lived in that large blue Victorian facing the Town Square, the same one Maddy had grown up in.

School had been let out following the teacher's death. But Police Chief Jim Purdue – Uncle Jim, to Aggie – had interviewed her and the other witnesses before letting them go for the day. School would be suspended for the rest of the week, as a sign of mourning.

The facts seemed cut and dry: An intruder shot a teacher at point-blank range. No one knew the motive. The alleged murderer was in police custody.

"Why do they say *alleged* murderer?" sobbed Aggie. "I saw him do it."

"There, there, dear," said her grandmother. "That's just legal talk. Ask your father." Aggie's dad had been a lawyer before being elected town mayor.

Principal Fred Zwicky released a statement expressing the school's sorrow in the loss of its teacher. "We will not tolerate killers walking the halls of our schools," he stated to reporters from the *Indianapolis Star* and the *Burpyville Gazette*. "In the days to come we will be doing even more to increase our school security."

Mayor Mark Tidemore – Aggie's dad – added, "Thank goodness, all our children are safe."

Tilly Tidemore had been reluctant to let Maddy and her friends swarm around Aggie so soon after the "incident." Aggie needed some quiet time. But Tilly knew there was no saying "no" to her mom.

"You poor dear –" Maddy was saying.

"I'm all right, Grammy. Truly I am."

"Your teacher, what was his name – Martin Scorsese?" asked Bootsie, not much of a cinephile. Her husband had mentioned the victim being Martin Something-or-another.

"Martin Lorenzo Griffith," corrected Lizzie. First thing, upon hearing the news, she had looked him up on Wikipedia. "He directed an indie film called *Four Weddings and a Funeral*."

"*Three Weddings and a Funeral*," Maddy corrected Lizzie's correction. Remembering her earlier conversation with her granddaughter about the film class.

"It was a prequel," Aggie said. "An unauthorized one."

"Unauthorized – what's that mean?" Cookie wanted to know.

"That the filmmakers didn't have the rights. The original film's producers sued them. That's why the movie got withdrawn from theatrical release."

"Oh."

"It's horrible," Aggie repeated. Tears streaming down her slightly freckled face.

"That the film was pulled from theaters?" asked Lizzie.

"No, that Marty is dead."

"You poor dear," Maddy hugged her.

"She needs to go upstairs and lay down," interjected Tilly. All this attention was just making matters worse. It had to be very traumatic, seeing your teacher assassinated right there in front of you. Experiences like this could result in PTSD or other psychological traumas. Thank goodness, the school was going to provide grief counseling. A shrink from Burpyville Memorial would be meeting twice a week with students who witnessed the murder.

"Marty was such a talented teacher," the girl continued with heaving sobs. "We were going to make a feature film as our class project."

"A film?" asked Lizzie.

"Yes, a rethinking of *The Wizard of Oz*. I was going to star as Dorothy. It might have been my big break."

"Oh, I know that movie. The one with the tornado that carries off a midwestern farm girl to the Emerald City of Oz." The 1939 MGM musical was one of Lizzie's very favorite musicals. She watched it on television every year.

"We were going to rent a wind machine for the tornado scenes."

"A wind machine?"

"A big fan," explained Aggie. "The kind that F/X crews use to simulate storms in Hollywood movies. We found one in Indy that we could rent by the day. We wanted to go for realism. Tornados can have winds of 250 MPH, you know."

"Why did that man shoot your teacher?" asked Bootsie, getting straight to the point. A cop's wife to the very core.

Aggie shook her head, blonde locks swaying. "Nobody knows. He just stepped into the classroom, yelled, 'Death to tyrants!' and started shooting."

"'Death to tyrants!' – that's what John Wilkes Booth shouted after assassinating Abraham Lincoln," noted Maddy.

"Actually, John Wilkes Booth said '*Sic semper tyrannis*," Cookie told them. Her eidetic memory on display. She had the ability to recall the contents of every book she'd ever read, a talent possessed by less than 1% of the population. "It's Latin for 'Thus always to tyrants.'"

"Was your teacher a tyrant?" asked Maddy. Trying to make sense of a senseless event.

"Martin Lorenzo Griffith was a hard grader," admitted Aggie, "but he certainly wasn't a tyrant. I liked him a lot. A whole lot."

"I read on the Internet that he was a distant relative of D.W. Griffith, the director who gave us *Birth of a Nation*," added Lizzie. "Filmmaking must have been in his blood."

"Don't say 'blood,'" moaned the pale-faced girl. "There was blood all over the classroom." She shut her eyes as if trying to shut out the disturbing imagery.

"According to the coroner, he was hit twice," reported Bootsie. "One bullet nicked his heart. He died of internal bleeding. It only took seconds. He didn't suffer."

"Did anyone else get hurt?" inquired Maddy. Concern showing on her oval face. She reminded you of that movie star, Ellen Burstyn.

"No, just Marty – I mean, Mr. Griffith."

"What happen after the man shot your teacher?" Bootsie wanted to know. Obviously, her husband Jim hadn't given her all the details.

"A couple of the football players tackled him. They'd disarmed him just as the school resource officer got to our classroom."

"How terrible to see someone killed before your very eyes," muttered Lizzie. Her own green eyes as wide as gooseberries, imagining the incident.

"I'll never forget the look on Mr. Griffith's face when he saw the man with the gun. It was like he'd seen a ghost."

"Who was the killer?" asked Maddy.

Aggie's chin trembled. "Like I told the deputy, it was that actor – Robert De Niro."

~ ~ ~

The radio announcer intoned: *"Earlier today a series of tornados swept across Missouri and Southern Illinois. Homes were damaged near the town of Bottlesburg. Three people were seriously injured. These twisters occur when warm, humid air from the equator meets cool, dry air from Canada and the Rockies. This swath of the Midwest is sometimes referred to as Tornado Alley. Here in Indiana we rank sixteenth among states with the most tornados per 10,000 square miles. So be careful out there and keep your eyes on the horizon ..."*

Lucius Plancus resented having to deliver the 3 o'clock weather report. He considered himself a crusading journalist, not a meteorologist. But here he was, reading today's weather off a computer screen in WZUR's Studio B.

A large, florid-faced redhead, Plancus was filling in for a sick colleague. However, this extra duty wasn't in his contract. He'd been hired as an "on-air reporter," to quote the signed document. Weighing over 300 pounds, he was an unsightly guy. His career would forever be relegated to radio, not television.

Being that he was 6-foot-2, it's not surprising that others at the radio station called him The Jolly Red Giant behind his back. But there was nothing jolly about him. He was a dour man, serious of purpose. And that serious purpose did not include talking about the damn weather.

~ ~ ~

"No, no, no," said Police Chief Jim Purdue to his wife and her friends. "Not *that* Robert De Niro. The killer was Robert Di Nero, a completely different spelling from the famous actor."

"Oh, thank goodness," exclaimed Lizzie. "I thought De Niro might be having a flashback to that earlier movie of his, *Taxi Driver*. You know, the one where he went berserk and shot everyone who came near his taxi cab."

"What would a big-time Hollywood actor like Robert De Niro be doing here in Caruthers Corners, Indiana?" chided Edgar Ridenour. The retired bank president was used to his wife gushing over movie stars and celebrity gossip. Most of the time he ignored her prattling about who Jennifer Aniston was marrying or Brad Pitt divorcing.

"Well, Martin Lorenzo Griffith was here. And he's a famous Hollywood director," said Bootsie.

"Hardly," countered Cookie. "I looked him up. Martin Griffith directed only one independent film. It was financed by a group of dentists out of Toledo. The movie was a total flop. So he gave up his film career and went into teaching."

"Oh my, don't tell Aggie that," cautioned Maddy. "She worshipped him."

"I think our Aggie had a little crush on her teacher," suggested Lizzie.

"Hey, she's going on sixteen," said Ben Bentley. "It's to be expected."

"I remember having a crush on our History teacher," said his wife Cookie. All eight of them – Cookie and Ben, Lizzie and Edgar, Bootsie and Jim, Maddy and Beau – had gone to school together. They had been best friends ever since – mostly.

"You're talking about Justin Ford Harribald?" teased Jim Purdue. "He was plump and bald, as I recall."

They gave everyone a good laugh. Pot calling the kettle black, for Jim was himself plump and nearly bald. He looked like that actor who plays Uncle Daddy on the *Claws* TV series.

"Mr. Harribald? Is that why you got interested in history?" Beau asked. Cookie was executive director of the Caruthers Corners Historical Society, the organization that shared quarters with the Perricock Museum of Science and History in that big stone mansion on a hill overlooking the town.

"Lordy no," the pale blonde laughed. "My grandfather got me interested in local history, with all his stories of olden times."

"Then what was your interest in Mr. Harribald?" queried Jim. But he thought he knew the answer.

"Mr. Harribald had a certain *je ne sais quoi*," giggled Cookie, sounding like a schoolgirl again.

"I think I *sais quoi*," said her husband Ben. "Justin Harribald had an eye for pretty students. As you'll recall, Cookie was a cheerleader back then. She was teacher's pet."

"It was all quite innocent," she blushed.

"Says you," Bootsie rolled her brown eyes.

The four families were having a cookout in the Madison's backyard that evening. They had planned it for weeks, kind of an end-of-summer gathering. Nobody was about to let a little thing like today's murder spoil it. Jim Purdue was happy to be off duty.

The backyard was wide and surrounded by shrubbery and illuminated by strings of white LED lights. The big Victorian house loomed over it like a gray wooden monolith. She and Beau had lived here for over thirty years. Over there was the tree where Freddie – that young daredevil – had fallen and broke his arm. Next to the fence was the spot where Bill buried his first dog, hit by a car. Here was the garden where Tilly planted her sunflowers, a canvas of Vincent Van Gogh yellows. And this was the paver-stone grill that Beau had built with his own hands, smoke curling over it as he barbecued tonight's high-protein fare. Maddy loved her home. It was a wonderful place to gather with her friends and family.

However, Aggie wasn't here tonight to enjoy the hot dogs and hamburgers. Tilly and Mark had taken their daughter to eat at a new pizza place down near Pitsville. The idea was to get her mind off today's shooting. Cheesy Pizza & Fun Emporium featured a wall lined with arcade games that operated on slugs instead of quarters. Each 16" pizza came with a bowl filled with two-dozen lead slugs stamped CHEESY PIZZA, good for an evening of video games.

A neat outing, thought Aggie. But it would have been even better if her three irritating little sisters hadn't been along. She liked it better when she'd been an only child.

CHAPTER THREE

Marie Daugherty Webster

Earlier that week Cookie had come across a first edition of *Quilts: Their Story and How to Make Them* by Marie D. Webster. Published in 1915, this was the first-ever American book about quilting.

She'd found the book in a trunk in the attic of an elderly lady who passed away last month. The woman had been a veritable pack rat, her house stuffed with Hummel figurines, dozens of old 33 1/3 phonograph records, several pieces of Johann Friedrich Böttger porcelain, a collection of crochet bed dolls, cabinets filled with assorted knickknacks, and rows upon rows of cluttered bookcases. Her estate had offered to donate anything of interest to the Historical Society.

Cookie was excited about finding a first edition of *Quilts: Their Story and How to Make Them*. A popular tome, it had been reprinted in 1916, 1926, 1928, 1929, 1943, 1948, and 2009, so a collector was more likely to find a later edition rather than a pristine, perfectly preserved 1915 volume.

As a member of the Quilters Club, Cookie was familiar with Marie Daugherty Webster (1859 - 1956). Mrs. Webster had been inducted into the Quilters Hall of Fame in 1991. Her family home in Marion, Indiana, was designated a National Historic Landmark and now served as headquarters for the Quilters Hall of Fame.

Although Marie Webster learned hand sewing from her mother, she didn't start designing quilts until well into her 50s. Inspired by the Arts and Crafts Movement, her appliqué quilts were known for their pastel floral designs. Today, her quilts are displayed in museums. As a matter of fact, the Indianapolis Museum of Art holds the largest collection of her quilts in the world.

The Quilters Club recently made a pilgrimage to Indy to view the Marie Webster quilts. After much negotiation, Lizzie Ridenour had managed to borrow one of them for an exhibit at the Hoople Quilting Heritage Museum. The visiting quilt – Marie Webster's 1925 "Pink Dogwoods in Appliqué" – was an early floral basket design celebrated for its "simplicity, quiet beauty, and restrained elegance."

This was quite a coup.

And now she had access to an original copy of Marie Webster's book.

The Quilters Club – including Aggie – gathered at the quilting museum to examine the find. The book looked practically new. They *ooo*'ed and *ahh*'ed over its delicate color illustrations. It had been autographed on the flyleaf by *Marie D. Webster* herself!

Lizzie asked if she could display it along with "Pink Dogwoods in Appliqué." No problem, nodded Cookie. They agreed the exhibit of a Marie Webster quilt would put the little museum on the map.

~ ~ ~

The Indianapolis Museum of Art has about two dozen Marie Daugherty Webster quilts. Identified by their designs, the quilts in the collection include such floral patterns as "Iris," "Morning Glory," "Nasturtium Wreath," "Cherokee Rose," "Sunflower," and "Daisies."

"Pink Dogwood" was one of Lizzie's favorites. An 83" x 83" scalloped-edge appliqué cotton quilt, the design featured four green baskets framing strands of pink dogwood blossoms. Marie Webster created it in 1925. The pattern was later published in the September 1927 issue of *Ladies' Home Journal*, where it was identified as part of the Webster Family Collection. This floral basket design also was widely circulated in the needlework journal, *Needlecraft*.

~ ~ ~

Marie Webster, née Marie Daugherty, did not start making appliqué quilts until about 1905. Unable to find a pattern that she liked, she designed one of her own. Inspired by her garden, the first design she came up with was a variation on the traditional "Rose of Sharon" pattern (which she renamed "American Beauty Rose").

About five years later *Ladies' Home Journal*, the leading women's magazine of the day, was actively soliciting new ideas from readers so she sent a design to its editor, Edward Bok. An Arts and Crafts advocate, he invited her to submit some designs for a full-color feature. She sent patterns for her "Pink Rose," "Iris," "Snowflake," and "Wind Blown Tulip" quilts. Published in the January 1, 1911, issue of the *Journal*, these four innovative designs were viewed by more than one-and-a-half million women. Overnight, Marie Webster became a national celebrity.

In 1915, Marie Webster published *Quilt: Their Story and How to Make Them*. And she continued to publish quilt designs in *Ladies Home Journal* for the next twenty years. The demand for her patterns became so great that soon she was filling orders from her home in Marion, Indiana.

In 1921 she started a mail-order pattern business, The Practical Patchwork Company. This enterprise was run from her home with the help of family and friends. The pattern packets, costing 50-cents each, included a photo of the quilt, brief directions, and fabric swatches, along with full-size blueprints and colored tissue-paper guides showing how to arrange the leaves and petals.

A quilting legend was born.

Her floral appliqué designs, created at the height of the Arts and Crafts movement, are still widely appreciated and imitated today.

CHAPTER FOUR

Catch and ...

Deputy Pete Hitzer had been the one who actually arrested the shooter at the high school. The school resource officer – an old-timer named Mortimer Remus – was little more than a crossing guard with a gun. Ol' Morty had dropped his pistol and raised his hands when the murderer of Martin Lorenzo Griffith pointed a Ruger SP101 at him and warned, "Stay where you are."

Thankfully, the football players came to his rescue.

Petie Hitzer got to the school within 10 minutes of the shooting. He walked into the classroom with his service revolver drawn and shouted, "Drop your weapon or I'm gonna put a bullet between your eyes. I won't ask twice."

No need to ask at all.

Robert Di Nero lay on the floor, with two high school linebackers sitting on top of him. "Don't shoot," he said in a quavering voice. "I give up."

~ ~ ~

Beau Madison and his pal Edgar Ridenour went fishing most weekends. Edgar owned a flat-bottomed jon boat that was perfect for catching catfish on the muddy Wabash. They missed Beau's grandson. Little N'yen was their fishing buddy. But he'd gone back to Chicago to join his parents. He'd lived with his Grammy and Grampy the past year or so when Kathy and Bill had been separated. But now the family was back together. The two men looked forward to the boy's next visit.

N'yen held the record – he'd caught Big Calvin, the elusive catfish in that hole near the bridge. Of course, they had let the big fellow go. Catch and release, that was the rule.

Beau was a tall beanpole, his pointed chin clean-shaven, his hair neatly trimmed. He was a regular at Snippets Inc. Head barber Gabe Hilty kept him well groomed. He looked the way a former mayor of the town should look – well-groomed and distinguished.

Edgar was just the opposite. After retiring from the Caruthers Corners Savings & Loan, he chucked his three-piece suits, quit shaving, and let his wispy circle of hair grow into a tangled bird's nest. His bushy beard and shaggily gray locks made him look more like an early fur trader than a former bank president. Sitting there on the boat, he could have passed as a rugged frontiersman like, say, Pierre La Plante, that early settler who traded with the "Pottawattamies" at Fort Harrison around 1820. Or John B. Duret, an agent of the American Fur Company, who bought pelts from the Indians at a spot on the southern bank of the Wabash around the same time.

A big bear of a man, Edgar Ridenour remained on several local boards despite his fearsome new appearance – Caruthers Corners Savings & Loan, Burpyville Memorial, Sons of Anthony Wayne, you name them.

"How's Aggie taking the death of her teacher?" asked Edgar as they drifted with the river in the aluminum boat. Nothing was biting today.

"Pretty hard. Not only did she really like the teacher, but she witnessed that crazy guy shoot him. Blood all over the place."

Edgar looked up through the lattice of trees. The sun was at its zenith. "I was talking with Fred Zwicky this morning –" he said.

"The school principal?"

Edgar nodded. "Yeah, you know Fred, don't you?"

"I've met him. He was a pain in the butt when I was mayor."

"Well, Fred was telling me that he's looking into how that Robert De Niro guy got inside the school with a gun. They've had a metal detector at the entrance for nearly two years now."

"That *is* a puzzle. Keeping guns out is the very reason the town council appropriated $10,000 to buy two of those gizmos – Garrett PD 6500i Metal Detectors – one for the high school and another for the elementary school."

"You think it was some kinda inside job?"

"Don't see how," Beau shook his head. "Teachers and administrators have to pass through that metal detector just like the students do."

"What we need are more security officers."

"You're right as rain about that. A study we commissioned back when I was mayor showed that a proper weapon detection program would require six security officers for approximately two hours each morning. An officer to run the initial portal metal detector, an officer to run the baggage X-ray machine, an officer to run the secondary portal metal detector for students who fail the initial detector, two officers (a male and a female) to operate the hand scanners on students who fail the secondary metal detector, and an officer to keep the students flowing smoothly and quickly through the system. We've got one guy."

"Yeah, Morty Remus. The guy must be a hundred years old."

"Fact is, we can't afford six officers for a school with 474 students. But we do need at least three."

"True," Edgar agreed. "Next time a shooter may be gunning for students. There have been 31 people killed in school shootings in the US since the beginning of the year."

"I just read that twice as many students have been killed in school shootings this year as have members of the military who were on deployment."

"Scary times."

"That's for sure. As a matter of fact, I think we – wait a minute! I've got a catfish on the line and he feels big as a whale!"

"Okay, careful now. Just work him easy."

"Catch and release?"

"Sure, that's how it works – catch and release."

~ ~ ~

Lucius Plancus walked into the station manager's office without knocking. Given his bulk, the big redhead was an intimidating presence. "I quit!" he said without waiting for his boss to look up from the programming schedules on his desk.

"W-what?" stuttered Clyde Carson.

"You heard me," bellowed Plancus. "I'm a broadcast journalist, not a weather reader."

"So —?" The station manager wasn't following the conversation. The man looming over him looked like the storybook giant preparing to chase Jack down the beanstalk.

"This is the second day I've filled in for that stupid weather guy. Enough!"

"But Jeffrey's been out sick — diverticulitis. Somebody has to deliver the weather report. Our listeners expect it."

Plancus' face was nearly as red as his hair. He looked like a stick of Wylie Coyote's Acme dynamite ready to explode. "Maybe so, but they don't expect it from me. I'm the guy who delivers the hard-hitting news. I should be covering that school shooting over in Caruthers Corners. Telling our audience why that teacher got shot."

"Kenny's covering that story."

"Hmph. Kenny couldn't deliver a story about a murder even if he were the victim."

CHAPTER FIVE

A Murder to Investigate

Let me out of here!" shouted Robert Di Nero. The stocky man shook the bars of the holding cell. He looked panicky. But that's understandable when you're under arrest for murder.

Myrtle Dobbler ignored him as she talked into the radio, coordinating between the chief and the two deputies on duty.

"C'mon, I demand my phone call. Everybody gets one phone call. That's the law, right?"

Myrtle paused to look in his direction. "Hush up, will you? I'm trying to work in here." She studied the guy's face. It was broad, the eyebrows heavy. He had a full head of dark, wavy hair. His jaw sported a five o'clock shadow, even though it was fairly early in the day. He looked more like a young Robin Williams than like the aging *Raging Bull* star.

"C'mon, lady. Give me my phone call. I want to get out of here!"

She removed her Keyblu Police headset to massage her temples. "You don't want to be locked up, don't go killing our schoolteachers."

"Marty deserved it. He ruined my career."

"What career's that?" She was getting aggravated by all his interruptions.

"Acting, of course."

27

"You gonna be an actor, I'd choose another stage name. Robert De Niro's already taken."

"My name's Di Nero, not De Niro. The *i*'s and *e*'s reversed."

"Ain't a big difference. Just sayin'." The dispatcher swiveled back to her radio and adjusted the earpiece.

"Yes, but –"

"Hush now," Myrtle cut him off. Turning the dial on her radio. "I gotta get back to work, Mr. Whatever Your Name Is."

"Robert Di Nero – that's my name," the man in the cell insisted.

"I'll believe that when I see your birth certificate," Myrtle snapped at him. "For all I know, you was born in Kenya."

~ ~ ~

Life had been good that summer for the Quilters Club. The gals and their husbands were "operating on cruise control," as Aggie's mom described it to a friend.

Cookie and Ben were fostering a 10-year-old boy, Gus Ritchie from Crackleton Corners. Bootsie and Jim had adopted three dogs. Maddy and Beau may as well have adopted Aggie, being their granddaughter spent so much time at her Grammy and Grampy's house. Lizzie bought herself a Panthère de Cartier pink gold watch and Edgar got a new Shimano Stradic FK Spinning Reel from L.L. Bean. Everybody was happy.

Aggie and her cousin N'yen had been in constant contact by telephone after he returned to Chicago to live with his parents. The brainy Vietnamese boy had come up with an algorithm that predicted habitable planets around G2V type stars. She didn't understand all his gobbledygook, but it sounded impressive. He was in touch with the Yerkes Observatory, a facility of the Department of Astronomy and Astrophysics at the University of Chicago. They had offered him an internship. Not bad for a 13-year-old kid.

The beginning of the school year had been – as Aunt Cookie liked to say – easy peasy. She loved her Film Appreciation class ... until that madman shot her teacher.

The death of Marty Griffith had been earth-shaking.

Aggie had been campaigning for the Quilters Club to look into it. However, her Grammy seemed ready to write the incident off. The death of the film teacher was a no starter. No mystery here. Everybody knew who killed him.

Just not why.

~ ~ ~

Fortunately, Aunt Lizzie had a sympathetic ear. "Girls, I think we ought to look into the murder of Aggie's film teacher," she announced when the four friends met for coffee at Cozy Café that morning.

"Why?" asked Maddy. She was blowing on her coffee to cool it off.

"Because it's important to Aggie."

Lizzy had sort of appointed herself as Aggie's mentor. For the past two years she'd been teaching the girl the sewing techniques that had netted the redhead four first-place awards in previous Watermelon Days quilting competitions. Lizzie was that good.

"But we don't normally do murders," argued Maddy. The Quilters Club had something of a reputation for being amateur sleuths. But most of their cases had involved quilts with mysterious messages, lost boys, haunted mansions, and money swindles. No murders.

"That's not entirely true," responded Lizzie. "Recently, we solved the case of that man thrown out of an airplane by a mob goon."

"And the one where those Russian spies were killing people with radiation poisoning," said Cookie.

"Don't forget, we also caught Evers Gochnauer's killer," added Bootsie. The police chief who replaced her husband Jim when he retired was already dead. Now Jim was back on the job, wearing the POLICE CHIEF badge. But that was only temporary – maybe.

"Hey, are all of you ganging up on me?" demanded Maddy. Looking at them sternly. "I'm as concerned about Aggie as anyone. I'm her blood relative, for gosh sakes."

"Jim won't like it, but I think we need to do this ," said Bootsie. "We owe it to Aggie." Her husband always objected to their meddling in police business. Despite their success rate in catching bad guys.

Maddy leaned back to eye her friends carefully. "We already know who the murderer is. A guy called Robert Di Nero – he's in the holding cell at the police department. There are a dozen witness, the entire Film Appreciation class."

"Yes," said Bootsie, "but we don't know *why* he did it."

"So have your husband ask him."

"Do you think Robert Di Nero will tell him?"

"Don't the police have ways of making people talk?" retorted Maddy. "You know, a rubber hose or a blackjack."

"Really!" sighed Bootsie. "The police don't do stuff like that. At least, Jim doesn't."

"The CIA has ways of making people talk," offered Lizzie. An avid reader of lurid spy novels. "They use sodium pentothal and waterboarding and batteries hooked to someone's private parts."

"Lizzie! You have to quit reading those Robert Ludlum books about James Bond."

"James Bourne," the redhead corrected her friend.

Maddy took a deep breath, then exhaled. "What does this have to do with the murder of Martin Lorenzo Griffith?"

"That's the question – why would someone shoot a lowly film teacher?"

"There are a few film critics I'd love to shoot," said Lizzie. She tended to be outspoken. "Those five-star reviews for *Batman v Superman* were totally misleading."

"It was better than *Batman & Robin*," opined Cookie.

"How can you say that?" responded Bootsie. "That one starred George Clooney."

Cookie wasn't buying it. "Clooney wore a Batman costume with built-in nipples," she pointed out. "Everybody says it was the worst Batman movie ever!"

"Well, yeah –"

"Ladies!" snapped Maddy, getting their attention. "We'll go down to the police department and speak with Robert Di Nero – if Jim will allow it. Ask him why he shot Aggie's teacher."

"– her favorite teacher," amended Lizzie.

"I'm not sure what knowing the answer will accomplish," sighed Maddy. "But let's do it so we can get back to our Community Quilt project."

CHAPTER SIX

Lawyering Up

J. Harold Wentworth was a shady lawyer based in Burpyville – at least for the moment. The Indiana State Bar Association was in the process of canceling his license to practice. Charges had already been filed against him for escrow fraud. He was little more than an ambulance chaser on his last run when he got the phone call from a man claiming to be Robert De Niro.

"The actor?"

"Yes, how did you know?"

"The name."

"Oh, I'm not that one. I'm Robert Di Nero, the *i* and the *e* reversed."

"You're kidding?"

"No, really. I'm the guy who shot that schoolteacher down in Caruthers Corners."

"Hold on," said Wentworth quickly. "Don't be making admissions of guilt over an open telephone line. The cops are probably listening."

"It doesn't matter. There were more than a dozen eyewitnesses. No question but that I did it."

"Then what can I do for you?"

"Get me off. I hear you have ways."

"Well –"

"I got a wad of money to pay you. Be worth your while."

"How much?"

"Twenty grand."

There came a pause as J. Harold Wentworth considered the offer.

Di Nero broke the silence. "I could probably go to twenty-five."

"Okay," said the lawyer. Liking the number. "I'll handle it."

~ ~ ~

"Thanks," said Robert Di Nero, handing the phone through the bars to Myrtle Dobbler.

"That's your one phone call," said the police dispatcher. "Hope you used it wisely. I've had some idiots use it to order pizza."

"Pizza? That sounds good. Do I get any lunch in here?"

"Sure you do. Comes over from Cozy Café next door. I think today's frank and beans day – lucky you."

"Van Camp's Pork and Beans? My favorite. They were invented in Indianapolis, you know."

Myrtle glanced at the clock on the wall. "Hang on. Lunch will be sent over in about a half hour."

~ ~ ~

"Hello. This is Johnny, Johnny Wentworth," said the voice on the phone.

"What do you want?" snapped Judge Bristol. "I told you I can't help with those disbarment proceedings. That's in the hands of the State Bar Association. Outta my reach."

"This is not about that. I've got a quick ten grand for you if you can get a client of mine out of jail."

"How would I do that?"

"I was thinking a Writ of Habeas Corpus."

"Who's this client?"

"A guy named Robert Di Nero. At least that's the name he's booked under."

"I've heard about him. That's a murder charge."

"So?"

"Murder's more difficult. I'll take some heat. Are you sure ten's all you can afford?

"Fifteen then."

"Okay, but this is the last one. Don't call me again."

"Not likely. The disbarment proceeding are scheduled for next week. Do you need a paralegal in your office? I wouldn't have to have a law license to do that."

"Boy, I wouldn't hire you to sweep the floor. Send me the fifteen and you'll get your Writ."

"Thanks." That left $10- of the $25,000 for him. Not bad for making a single phone call.

~ ~ ~

Lucius Plancus was doing the weather again. His threat to quit had not gotten him anywhere.

> *"More tornados touched down today in Southern Illinois and Indiana. Two house trailers were destroyed near the town of Twinsburg, just on this side of the Indiana border. No one was injured due to the inhabitants being at work ...."*

When the segment was over, he turned to the station manager, who was sitting next to him in WZUR's Studio B. "How's Jeffrey's tummy ache? Will he be getting back to the station anytime soon? I don't plan on reading the weather forever."

"Who knows. But I sure hope so. We're practically running on a skeleton crew." He'd been working the controls, because the sound engineer had phoned in sick. The flu, he claimed.

"Hire somebody. I don't like doing the weather. I want to cover that teacher's murder up in Caruthers Corners."

"I told you, Kenny has that covered."

"Kenny's getting nowhere with that story. He doesn't know anything about the killer ... the guy's motive ... the backstory on the victim. He's got nothing."

"Well, you're right about that. Maybe I ought to pull Kenny in to do the weather and give you a crack at that murder story."

"Now you're talking!"

CHAPTER SEVEN

... Release

Police Chief Jim Purdue was surprised to discover his murder suspect had been sprung by a slick lawyer who'd somehow managed to bamboozle Judge John Lawrence Bristol into issuing a Writ of Habeas Corpus.

"Sorry, Chief. I didn't have any choice when that shyster marched in here with a Writ signed by Judge Bristol. Myrtle even called the judge's chambers to confirm he'd really signed it."

The Chief merely shrugged and said, "Don't worry about it, Petie. Somebody else will bust him. Bad guys don't change."

Catch and release.

One smelly fish back in the river.

But later that afternoon when the FBI came back with an identification on the fingerprints, Chief Purdue's interest in the prisoner returned. According to the Feebies, the collection of arches, loops, and whorls belonged to someone named Robert Dietrich Black.

"Odd," Jim Purdue said. "Why would the guy try to pass himself off as Robert De Niro?"

"He called himself Robert Di Nero, not Robert De Nero," corrected Myrtle Dobbler. "The *i* and *e* are reversed." She enunciated carefully to show the difference.

"You say tomato, I say tomahto."

"I've never heard you say tomahto," said Deputy Petie Hitzer. Puzzled by the apparent *non sequitur*.

Chief Purdue sighed. "I'm just saying it beats me why he'd pick that name to use as an alias."

It was the Quilters Club who figured it out.

~ ~ ~

That evening the four families went out for dinner at the Pizza Hut up on Highway 21. Bootsie was fond of their Super Supreme Pizza -- a combo of pepperoni, ham, beef, pork sausage, Italian sausage, red onions, mushrooms, green peppers and black olives – 3,440 calories in all. Bootsie could eat an entire pie by herself.

To the contrary, Lizzie ate like a bird. She always ordered the Naked Wings. Chicken with no sauce. 162 calories for two wings. No wonder she was so skinny.

The menfolk were hungry. Since a large 14" pizza offered eight slices, they added two more pies – three in all. That afforded three slices each for the boys, two each for Maddy and Cookie, and a whole pie for Bootsie.

In truth, Bootsie did not eat all eight slices on the spot. She took three home in a doggie bag, saving them for a midnight snack. She loved cold pizza.

As they were noshing, Jim told them about the true identity of the man who shot that teacher. They loved it when the police chief gave them "inside information."

Jim said, "The guy claimed he was Robert Di Nero, spelled slightly different than the *Raging Bull* actor. But it turns out the FBI identified him as somebody called Robert Dietrich Nero. I don't get it. Was he trying to pass himself off as the Oscar-winning movie star? If so, he should learn to spell better."

"Obviously an alias," said Bootsie between bites. Her cheeks bulged like a chipmunk's.

"I'd say it was more of a stage name," agreed Maddy. She was chewing slowly and deliberately, as was her manner.

"I've got it," announced Cookie, picking the olives off her pizza. She never did like those bitter little black fruits. "Robert is his given name. Dietrich, he abbreviated to 'Di.' And Nero is Italian for 'black,'" she broke the code. "Robert Dietrich Black and Robert Di Nero are essentially the same name."

"Hmph," said Edgar. "Why use two names?"

"Actors often do," shrugged Lizzie. She kept up on Hollywood gossip. She could tell you that Woody Allen's birth name was Allan Stewart Konigsberg. Or that Tom Cruise was born as Thomas Cruise Mapother IV.

"Hold on a minute," said Maddy, pulling out her iPhone. "I've got an IMDb app on here."

"What's that?" asked her husband.

"Internet Movie Database," said Cookie. Drawing on her super memory. "The IMDb lists approximately 4.7 million titles and 8.3 million personalities in its database. Movies, TV shows, episodes, actors, directors."

By now, Maddy had connected to her little yellow-and-black app. "R-O-B-E-R-T," she began typing in the name. "Hmm," she said, "nothing listed here for Robert Dietrich Black."

"Oh well," said Jim Purdue. "It was an interesting thought."

"Just a minute," repeated Maddy, trying again. "R-O-B-E-R-T," she typed.

"Anything?" prodded Lizzie, trying to look over her friend's shoulder.

"Hold on. Yes, here. An actor is listed under the spelling of ROBERT DI NERO."

"Are you sure it's not another variation for the *Raging Bull* guy?"

"No, this actor only has one movie credit to his name. An indie film called *Three Weddings and a Funeral*."

"Does it have a picture of him?"

"Yes, here."

"Bingo," said Jim Purdue. "That's our guy."

~ ~ ~

As the husbands split up the Pizza Hut check, Maddy turned to her gal pals, saying, "So much for our interviewing Robert Di Nero or whatever his name is. I can't believe Judge Bristol sprung him on a Habeas Corpus."

"Very strange," nodded Bootsie, packing away her extra pizza in her large Lauren Ashley shoulder bag. "I don't recall Jim ever losing a prisoner to a Writ before."

"Without Robert Whatever-his-name-is, I'm not sure where to go from here," admitted Cookie.

Lizzie looked pained, but it wasn't the green peppers on the pizza. "Does that mean we stop looking into the murder? Aggie will be very disappointed."

"I suppose we could keep poking at it a little," relented Maddy. A complete turnabout from her earlier position. "I don't like the idea of someone getting away with murder on a legal technicality."

"So what do we do?" asked Bootsie. Or maybe it was Lizzie.

"Mmmm," said Maddy. "Maybe it's time we watched that movie."

~ ~ ~

When they got home Beau went straight to bed. He had eaten his three slices of pizza plus one of Maddy's and felt, as he put it, "fat and happy."

Slender all his life, Beau could pack in all the food on the table and never gain an ounce. His wife, on the other hand, had to watch her calories. Like that nursery rhyme about Jack Splat.

Maddy didn't turn in right away. After pulling on her nightgown, she went into the den and powered up her MacBook Pro. The computer screen turned blue, then populated itself with folders and documents. She tapped the button for the Safari browser and watched the Google window open. In the horizontal box she entered the words ROTTENTOMATOES.COM and waited for the website to open.

Rotten Tomatoes is an aggregator of reviews by film critics. Each film's rankings are tallied and the site rates it as either Certified Fresh, Fresh, or Rotten – depending on its numeric score.

First up, Maddy checked out the 1994 Hugh Grant movie, *Four Weddings and a Funeral*. There it was, a rating on the Tomatometer of 95. Pretty impressive.

The critics liked it:

- *The Philadelphia Inquirer*'s Steven Rea observed, "*Four Weddings and a Funeral* is one of those rare films that have you smiling from the get-go, and keep you that way ... right to the end."

- Gene Siskel of *The Chicago Tribune* said, "Although the film is basically a light romantic comedy, it couldn't be more psychologically astute in its portrait of a man who defines himself by his bachelorhood, which empowers him to get past his fear of commitment."

- And Kenneth Turan wrote in *The Los Angeles Times*, "Deftly written by Richard Curtis and directed by the versatile Mike Newell, *Four Weddings* is as good as its word, breezily following a small circle of friends through every one of the events the title promises."

The words made her want to see the British comedy all over again.

Then she typed *Three Weddings and a Funeral* into the site's search box and up came a page displaying a splattered green tomato image at the top. The number next to it indicated a dismal score of 14 out of 100.

Down the page were comments by the critics:

- A squib from the review by Thomas Elgort of *The Boston Standard* said: "The acting in this abomination is so bad I'll be surprised if any of the cast ever works again."

- Abe Coulson of *Chicago Herald-Standard* added: "This rip-off of a British classic is an embarrassment to anyone connected to its production."

- And Tom Dinsdale of *San Francisco Sexton* summed it up: "The film's star, an unknown who goes by the stolen and mangled name of Robert Di Nero, steals the show ... and we hope he doesn't give it back. It's a shoddy mess!"

Harsh words indeed.

Three Weddings and a Funeral wasn't exactly a career-builder. One could imagine Robert Dietrich Black being very unhappy with the film's director. But enough to shoot him?

CHAPTER EIGHT

The Bad Movie

The next day Maddy assembled the Quilters Club in her comfy den. A 55-inch TCL 4K Ultra HD Roku television dominated the room. A family Christmas present from last year.

"We agreed that we should take a look at Martin Lorenzo Griffith's masterpiece," she announced.

"Grammy! Are you being sarcastic?"

"Sorry, Aggie."

"Let's reserve our judgment till after we watch it," suggested Cookie, always polite.

"Me for one, I can't wait to see it," said the girl.

"You're saying you've never seen *Three Weddings and a Funeral*?" responded Lizzie. Astonished that Aggie hadn't already screened this film by her cinematic idol.

"I was waiting. Marty promised to show it to the class after Thanksgiving break. He said he'd do a scene-by-scene commentary." The girl paused. "But that will never happen now," she added sadly.

"How did you get a copy of the film?" asked Bootsie.

Maddy nodded toward the television set. "This TV comes with Roku. I found the movie on the Roku Channel. Since the service is free, you find a lot of ... less popular films there." Maddy glanced at her granddaughter to see how she took that description. Everything appeared calm.

"Do you have any popcorn?" That came from Bootsie, of course.

"Okay, give me a minute to fire up the Presto Hot Air Popper."

"With butter?"

Ten minutes later – a bowl of hot buttered popcorn on the coffee table – they were watching the opening credits of *Three Weddings and a Funeral*.

The words filled the screen:

A FILM BY MARTIN LORENZO GRIFFITH

**Based on a Concept by Martin Lorenzo Griffith
Screenplay by Lloyd Frankenheimer
DIRECTED BY MARTIN LORENZO GRIFFITH**

That probably offered a clue as to why Robert Black was upset about the film. But 90 minutes later, everybody knew for sure.

The plot was about a shy guy (played by a dour Robert Di Nero) who meets a high-spirited bride's maid (the exuberant Missy Montana) at a Long Island wedding. It's not clear whose wedding it is, or why the guy is there. They bump into each other again at two more weddings, then get married at a funeral. It's not clear who had died. Or why they got married.

The acting was bad, particularly Di Nero's. The pacing was slow, the scenes too long. The storyline hard to follow. The lighting dark, the sound loud. The thing was a mess.

Everybody in the den had a hard time keeping from laughing or booing or making rude comments. It was like a *Mystery Science Theater 3000* without the riffing.

Aggie looked embarrassed when the room's lights came up. "Well, that was ... quite a show," she managed to squeak out.

Maddy pulled the blinds open. "That blonde, Missy Montana, she reminds me of someone. Wish I could remember who."

"Was that Martin Griffith who played the minister?"

"Uh, yes, that was Marty," nodded Aggie. "A small role, but he was busy directing the film."

"Are these supposed to be the same characters as in the British film?" asked Bootsie, all confused.

"I think these are supposed to be their American cousins. But it wasn't very clear, was it?" said the girl.

"I thought it was interesting," offered Lizzie. Lying, of course.

Cookie had nothing to add. Her mother had taught her, if you can't say anything good, say nothing at all.

"Oh, poo. You're all trying so hard to be nice," sighed Aggie. "Just go ahead and say it, the film was a stinker."

"The film was a stinker," said Maddy, patting her granddaughter's hand.

~ ~ ~

Turns out, the reason *Three Weddings and a Funeral* looked so crappy was because Martin Lorenzo Griffith had raked $200,000 off the top of the film's production budget, pocketing it for himself. There wasn't enough left to pay a decent editor, or do color corrections, or fix the sound. Therefore, a bad movie was made worse.

The discrepancy came to light when the investors demanded an audit. Unfortunately, dentists are better at pulling teeth than unraveling Hollywood accounting, so they were never really able to prove he stole the money.

And Marty walked away with $200 grand.

Robert Dietrich Black knew Marty had it. And he wanted his share. It was bad enough Marty had robbed Bobby of his co-directing credit, the jerk had taken all the money too.

But no one could find it.

A few weeks ago Bobby hired a private investigator. According to the PI's interim report, Martin Griffith had no bank accounts, no savings accounts, no brokerage accounts, no evidence of an offshore bank account, *nada*.

After the film flopped, Marty had continued to live a frugal lifestyle. Took a job as a schoolteacher at minimal wages. Drove a rattletrap Chevy. Carried his lunch to school in a paper bag. Left no signs that he had any money.

~ ~ ~

Odell Lumley was a licensed private investigator in Indy. However, he was not a hardboiled two-fisted gumshoe like those operatives you read about in books by Raymond Chandler and Dashiell Hammett. He was more of a computer nerd, most of his detective work taking place on the Internet. He was so good at it that he'd once tracked down a fugitive hiding in a tent in the Sahara Desert. Not bad, if he said so himself.

There are records for almost everybody: Driver's licenses, military records, electricity bills, parking tickets, passports and visas, fingerprint cards, book club memberships, magazine subscriptions, email accounts, FedEx deliveries, tax filings, Cheesy Pizza birthday clubs, you name it. It was just a matter of looking in the right place.

Lumley had been hired to take a look-see at a teacher over in a nearby town, a guy named Martin Lorenzo Griffith. According to the client, this Griffith fellow had walked off with $200,000 that belonged to somebody else. His client, presumably. His job was to find it.

After two weeks of diligent searching, Lumley had turned up nothing. Either Griffith didn't have the money ... or it was buried in a tin can in the backyard. There was absolutely no trace of the moolah.

His client wasn't happy with the report.

"What am I paying you a hundred bucks an hour to do?" Robert Di Nero had shouted. "To look at porn sites on your computer and then send me the bill?"

"Here's a list of where I've searched," said Lumley, handing him a sheaf of papers just coughed out of his Epson WorkForce Pro WF-R4640 printer. It was a lengthy column printed in 14 pt. Helvetica on Staples 22-lb. Bright White copy paper. Very organized. Lumley was a pro.

Di Nero angrily wadded the paper into a ball and threw it at him. "I know Marty has that money and I intend to get it – with your help or not."

"I've looked everywhere," said Lumley, keeping his cool. He got paid whether he found the money or not. "It's just not there. If he's got the money, he hasn't spent a penny of it. I've gone over his bank statements, his tax records, even his supermarket receipts." He turned around his Hewlett Packard ProBook 470 G5 with its Intel i7-8550U Quad-core to display the screen. "Here's his bank account with $32.87 in it. No savings account or CDs or retirement fund. He'll be hard-pressed to make it to his next paycheck."

"Well, if Marty doesn't have the money he's gonna wish he did." That's when Robert Di Nero stormed out.

That very day he climbed into his Nissan junker and drove over to Caruthers High to shoot his old college roommate.

Death to tyrants, he kept muttering to himself.

CHAPTER NINE

What About Martin?

Okay, let's face it. Agnes Tidemore had had a little crush on her teacher. That was normal enough for a teenage girl.

Martin Lorenzo Griffith had been quite handsome, with his cerulean-blue eyes and crooked smile and lion's mane of blond hair swept back over his ears. He looked more like a movie star than a high school teacher.

This was his first semester as an educator, teaching Film Appreciation 101 and Film Production 201. It was part of Caruthers High's new Vocational Studies program. The school had even purchased the equipment to let his class make a student film. The argument was, if the drama department could put on a school play, why not have the new film department make a movie?

Aggie had been thrilled when Marty had cast her as the lead – Dorothy in *The Wizard of Oz*. He promised to help her work on memorizing her lines. He was such a great guy.

Of course, Marty was no competition for her boyfriend Bobby Elwood. She knew Marty was – to steal that line from *The Maltese Falcon* – "the stuff that dreams are made of," a fantasy.

Sometimes when Bobby kissed her, she pretended it was Mr. Griffith.

That was harmless, wasn't it?

Aggie had been horrified when that stranger burst into the classroom and pumped a volley of bullets into her favorite teacher. Witnessing that had been truly traumatizing for the dozen students who witnessed the senseless murder. Each of them had been assigned to a grief counselor from Burpyville Memorial. But it hadn't really helped.

Aggie couldn't help but feel heartbroken. Marty had been so nice and kind and smart ... and handsome. Her fantasies of growing up and marrying him and moving to Hollywood and becoming a movie star were completely dashed. Besides, nobody from a dinky little town like Caruthers Corners could ever become a real movie star like you saw up there on the silver screen at the AMC Multiplex ... could they?

CHAPTER TEN

On the Case

The Quilters Club wasn't sure where to go next with the investigation of Martin Lorenzo Griffith's death. "Maybe we need to do more research," suggested Maddy.

So they divvied it up.

Cookie did a little background checking on both the victim and his killer.

Turns out, Martin Lorenzo Griffith was born in Santa Ynez, a historic cowboy town south of Los Angeles. His parents owned an orange grove. There was no evidence that he was related to early filmmaker D.W. Griffith, despite the claim on his IMDb bio.

Robert Dietrich Black had been born in Manchester, New Hampshire. His parents were now deceased. He had no siblings. In high school he'd been voted Most Likely to Work at Disneyland. He wore contact lens. He starred in the senior play, a production of *Equus*. He had a history of depression.

Black and Griffith met at Ball State University. Located on 1,140 acres in Muncie, Indiana, Ball State also has satellite campuses in Fisher and Indianapolis. They both minored in Film and Screenwriting. The boys had been roommates.

There they hooked up with another classmate, Lloyd Frankenheimer. A geeky guy from Toledo, Lloyd's uncle was an orthodontist who wanted to invest in a movie. Uncle Simon and a couple of other DMDs came up with a million bucks. In return, they were promised Executive Producer titles on Lloyd's proposed film (working title: *Graveside Wedding*), front-row seats at the premiere, and the chance to meet sexy movie starlets.

~ ~ ~

Bootsie cajoled her husband into doing a search on the National Crime identification Center (NCIC) database. He turned up an arrest for one Martin Lorenzo Griffith on the charge of theft, but the charges had been dropped for lack of evidence.

Under Indiana law (Indiana Code Title 35. Criminal Law and Procedure § 35-43-4-1) embezzlement is charged as a theft. The crime is described: "A person who knowingly or intentionally exerts unauthorized control over property of another person, with intent to deprive the other person of any part of its value or use, commits theft (theft in general)."

The claim was that Griffith had stolen approximately $200,000 from Graveside Productions, LLC, a film company set up by a group of investors out of Toledo. The production company had been incorporated in Indiana since that's where the filming took place.

A missing $200,000 – now that was interesting.

~ ~ ~

Lizzie spent three hours searching the online archives of *Variety* and *Hollywood Reporter* for any information about the movie. She turned up five related articles between the two publications.

The first squib announced that an indie studio was beginning production on a film titled *Graveside Wedding*.

The second noted that the working title of *Graveside Wedding* had been changed to *Three Weddings and a Funeral*.

The third was a notice that Missy Montana had been signed to star in *Three Weddings and a Funeral*.

Fourth was a notation that Oscar-winning actor Robert De Niro had filed a complaint with the Screen Actors Guild (SAG) about the appropriation of his name by another performer.

The fifth article was more expansive, detailing an injunction against Graveside Productions LLC by PolyGram Filmed Entertainment, Channel Four Films, and Working Title Films to stop the distribution of *Three Weddings and a Funeral* based on copyright infringement. The lawsuit cited similar name, similar plot, and passages of dialogue lifted directly from *Four Weddings and a Funeral*.

A defense of parody was turned down by the courts and the film was pulled from theatrical distribution.

~ ~ ~

Maddy consulted with her son-in-law, a lawyer by training. Mark the Shark pointed out that Robert Dietrich Black could still be brought to trial for murder if new evidence was brought forth. But this history of a business deal gone bad was not enough to do the trick. They needed something more.

What kind of new evidence would that be, a verbal confession?

~ ~ ~

Aggie had been excluded from the investigation for fear it might be emotionally upsetting for her to revisit the death of her teacher. That was just fine with Tilly. She'd never truly approved of her daughter's involvement in solving crimes with the Quilters Club. It was too dangerous for a 15-year-old girl to be chasing around after criminals.

Besides, the psychologist from Burpyville Memorial had recommended that the students not dwell on the murder they witnessed. "Emotional baggage," she described the trauma. "Toss it out. Get rid of the thoughts. Erase the bad memory."

In Cognitive Behavioral Therapy the goal is to help individuals identify thoughts that make them feel afraid or upset and replace them with less distressing thoughts. This therapist was definitely of the "think happy thoughts" school of CBT.

Aggie wasn't pleased with this advice. Or about being shut out by the Quilters Club from the investigation. If that was the way it was, Aggie decided, she'd just have to bring Robert Dietrich Black to justice on her own.

CHAPTER ELEVEN

Back to School

Aggie kept thinking about the murder of her teacher. First up, she was curious how Robert Di Nero got into the school building. In these uncertain times, getting into a school building was difficult. Only one entrance, a metal detector, backpack inspections, an armed resource officer on hand.

How did Robert De Niro get in? she wondered.

So she walked over to Caruthers High to examine the scene of the crime. That's what detectives did, wasn't it?

The school wasn't far, less than half-a-mile from her home. She knew the building was closed but hoped someone might be there – an administrator, a teacher, the janitor, maybe the school resource officer. But no. The entrance was locked up tight and a sign taped to the door announced SCHOOL CLOSED TILL FURTHER NOTICE. A result of the murder.

About two years ago, Caruthers High had reacted to reports of a school shooting in Roseburg, Oregon, where eight students died. The School Board authorized the installation of metal detectors and closing up all the entrances except for the main door. The school's opening had been moved to 7:20 a.m. to allow for the slow-down in admitting students.

Nevertheless, it was the job of the school resource officer to keep unauthorized people out. But somehow he had failed.

~ ~ ~

"Hi, Myrtle. This is Aggie Tidemore. Can you tell me where Mortimer Remus lives?"

"Why you want to know that, girl?" Her voice sounded suspicious over the telephone. Maybe it was a bad connection.

"I know Officer Remus from school. I want to ask him a couple of questions."

"About what?"

"The shooter who killed my teacher."

"That guy who calls himself Robert De Niro? We had him locked up in the holding cell less'n ten feet from where I'm sitting. But some high-powered lawyer waltzed in here with an order from Judge Bristol and sprung him."

"That's just not right. I *saw* him shoot Mr. Griffith."

"You an' me agree on that."

"So could you give me the address for Morty Remus – pretty please?"

"No way, girl. Chief Purdue would fire my fat butt if I give out personnel information like that."

"I could ask my father –"

"Don't you go playing the Daddy Card with me. That ain't gonna work, no way."

"Myrtle, do you want to see this guy Robert Di Nero get away with murder?"

"Course not."

"Then you need to help the Quilters Club bring him to justice. He's already slipped out of your hands."

"The Quilters Club, huh?"

"You know we've solved a few crimes that the police couldn't."

"Hey, we woulda caught most of them bad guys if given enough time."

"But we helped get them, for sure."

"Okay, okay, you win. Long as you're working with the Quilters Club."

"Yes, I am," she lied.

"Here, I'll give you Morty's address. But don't tell nobody you got it from me."

~ ~ ~

Morty Remus was the school resource officer assigned to the high school. Another guy had the elementary school. They worked as adjunct members of the Caruthers Corners Police Department, reporting to Chief Purdue. Their schedule had them supervising entry into the school each morning and patrolling the hallways during school hours.

Morty was 73 years old, a bit overweight, not at the peak of fitness. A little slow of pace, his reaction time was not what it used to be. Maybe he felt guilty that he'd allowed the shooter into the school.

As he explained it to Aggie when she dropped by his cottage at the foot of Hoople Hill, this guy De Niro had told him he was an old college roommate of Martin Lorenzo Griffith and wanted to surprise his pal with an unannounced drop-in.

"Why not? I thought," said Morty Remus. "He seemed like a nice kid."

"But that's against the rules," Aggie pointed out.

"I know, I know. Didn't even run his backpack through the scanner. I'm sure I'll lose my job over this. And I'll carry the guilt for that teacher's death with me the rest of my life. I was only trying to do something nice. And look how it turned out!"

Nulla actio impunita, as Aggie's Latin teacher used to say.

CHAPTER TWELVE

Chilly Willy

The man who walked into the Caruthers Corners Police Department looked like a parody of Danny DeVito in *Get Shorty* – barely 5-foot-tall, balding head with a fringe of frizzy hair, his body as rotund as Humpty Dumpty. While DeVito's character in the movie was a big-time Hollywood actor, this man introduced himself as Wilson "Chilly Willy" LaMont, a small-time talent agent out of Indianapolis.

"I need your protection," he announced. "Put me in one of those witness programs."

Chief Jim Purdue was taken aback. "W-we don't do that," he sputtered. "That's the Feds."

"If you don't do something, he's going to kill me," screamed LaMont. "I'm next on his list." He looked ridiculous, standing there in a tropical Tommy Bahama shirt and baggy Bermuda shorts. He was wearing flip-flops on his hairy feet as if this were sunny California.

"On whose list?" asked Chief Purdue. Looking around as if he expected a team of Ninjas to burst in the door.

"Bobby Black's list. I'm gonna be his next victim."

"You mean Robert Dietrich Black?"

"Yes. And if he kills me it will be *your* fault. You're the one who let that bloodthirsty murderer go free."

"Hey, we had no choice. We were following a court order," Chief Purdue held out his palms as if fending off the accusation. "The law's the law."

"Are you sure you can't put me in a witness protection program?"

"First, you're not a witness. And second, a small-town police department doesn't have programs like that."

"C'mon, I've seen it in movies. *Did You Hear About the Morgans? The Family. Madea's Witness Protection. Hide in Plain Sight.*"

"You're referring to the United States Federal Witness Protection Program that's administered by the Department of Justice and monitored by the US Marshal Service. The WITSEC program was established under Title V of the Organized Crime Control Act of 1970."

"States don't do it?"

"Some states have their own witness protection programs for crimes not covered by the federal program. Those states include, uh, New York, California, Connecticut, Texas, Illinois – but not Indiana."

Chilly Willy LaMont looked panicky. "What am I gonna do?"

"You're from Indy, you say? The Indianapolis City Council just earmarked $300,000 for a city witness protection program – but I doubt you'd qualify."

"That's not fair. Bobby Black is gunning for me. He's crazy as a bedbug."

Jim Purdue took a deep breath. "Tell me, why does he want to kill you?"

"Same reason he killed Marty Griffith. Because we put him in that meshuganah movie, *Three Weddings and a Funeral*."

"So what?"

"It ruined his career. And he blames us."

"You were his agent?"

"That's right. And Marty directed the film. Bobby doesn't seem to care that it ruined our careers too. Marty had to take a job teaching. No one would hire him to direct another film. And I lost half my clients. I had some big names too."

"Like who?" asked Petie Hitzer. The deputy was easily star struck.

"Eric Longbottom. Ace Dobbs."

"Never heard of them," said Chief Purdue. Not a big moviegoer to begin with. He and Bootsie were television watchers.

"Have you ever heard of James Dean?"

"Sure. But he's long dead."

"Yes, but I gave Jimmy his start. He was raised over here in Fairmount, Indiana, you know."

"Everybody knows that," said Petie Hitzer. "Is that where you discovered him?"

"You bet."

Chief Purdue wasn't so sure about that. According to what he'd read, James Dean didn't get interested in acting till he moved to California to live with his dad. He enrolled in a drama class at UCLA – 2,000 miles away from Chilly Willy LaMont's little talent agency in Indy.

"Let me make sure I've got this right," said the police chief. "Robert Dietrich Black is out to kill people

63

connected to this film, *Three Weddings and a Funeral?*"

"Right. He blames us for ruining his career. You better check on Lloyd Frankenheimer too. He wrote the screenplay."

"Anybody else?"

"Maybe Missy Montana – she was his co-star."

Petie's face lit up. "Missy Montana? She's a big-time movie star. I saw one of her pictures at the Multiplex over in Burpyville. A remake of *10*, with her in the Bo Derek role. I read that it was the number one comedy for five weeks in a row."

"That's what Bobby resents about Missy Montana – her success."

"Who did the Dudley Moore role?" asked Jim Purdue. But no one was listening to him.

~ ~ ~

Aggie stood in front of Caruthers High again, studying its rusty brick facade. Morty Remus had been very helpful, being that he was remorseful about his unintentional role in the teacher's murder. He had literally opened the door for the killer. Something that would haunt Morty for the rest of his life.

As instructed, Aggie walked around the corner of the school building to a side door that led into the gymnasium. It was locked from the inside. Nevertheless, she put her hand firmly around the knob, just as Morty Remus had told her to do, and yanked upward. *Click!* – the lock popped open. A trick that came with knowing the secrets of an aging building. Morty had worked there as a resource officer for close to ten years now, taking the job right after he retired from the Burpyville Police Department in '08. He knew the building inside and out.

She slipped into the dark gym and crossed the basketball court to a pair of wide double doors. These opened into a dimly lit hallway lined with green metal lockers. She walked toward the east wing of the school, trailing her fingers along the gray wall opposite the lockers. She recognized the door to her Film Appreciation classroom by the crisscrossing yellow tape that proclaimed CRIME SCENE CRIME SCENE CRIME SCENE.

Ducking under the tape, Aggie found that the door was unlocked. She stepped inside and switched on the lights. Being that there were no windows in this boxy classroom, passersby couldn't see the blazing fluorescents that now illuminated the crime scene.

She was looking for clues ... but had no idea what kind of clues. A man had shot her teacher. Obviously, Mr. Griffith wasn't expecting the violent act – she remembered the look of surprise on his face – so what kind of clue would there be? She walked around the parameter of the classroom, seeing nothing that looked interesting. She moved carefully, avoiding the rusty pools of dried blood. Finally, her attention focused on the bulky oak desk in the front of the room.

She examined the top of the desk: Tattered movie screenplays were stacked on one corner. The screenplay on top was "CHINATOWN" by Robert Towne. She didn't look at the others. On the other end of the desk lay a zebra-striped clapperboard – one of those devices that are banged in front of the camera as the director yells "Action!" A few pencils were scattered across the green blotter. The blotter must have been left over from a previous class for the doodling on it included such phrases as $E=MC^2$ and ARCHIMEDES SHOULD SOAK HS HEAD! An old science class, no doubt.

Next, she searched through the desk drawers. They smelled of chalk and rubber cement. The contents were varied: A brown paper lunch bag containing a stale ham sandwich in a Ziploc pouch. A sheaf of papers detailing Caruthers High rules and regulations. A few stray copies of the Film Appreciation class's syllabus. Files, one each for every student in the class.

Aggie couldn't resist looking: She had been making straight *A*'s in Film Appreciation 101. What would happen to that grade, now that the class had been canceled. Wasn't fair – but she'd probably lose it.

Finally, she checked the center drawer. It contained several No. 2 pencils and Bic ballpoint pens, a box of staples but no stapler, and a box of white chalk. Plus ticket stubs from the AMC Multiplex in Burpyville for a movie called *Papillion*, a recent remake of the Steve McQueen and Dustin Hoffman classic.

Aggie wasn't big on remakes. Like Mr. Griffith had told the class, if a movie was good, it didn't need to be remade. If it was bad, it didn't deserve to be remade. But Hollywood studios notoriously recycle ideas.

There, in a corner of the drawer, she spotted a scrap of paper with numbers scribbled on it: 2L-6R-2L. She recognized this as a locker combination. Being new this semester, Marty Griffith had written down his combination in case he forgot it.

Everybody in the school was assigned a locker, even the teachers. All the metal closets had a built-in combination lock. As it happened, Marty's locker was located two down from hers. She'd seen him at it every day of this semester. It always gave her a chance to talk with him, maybe flirt just a bit.

Carrying the slip of paper, she walked into the hallway and followed the worn tile down to her locker – 246 – then went two more. She tried the combination and – *snik!* – it opened just as expected. Inside she found a copy of his Film Appreciation class textbook – *The Liveliest Art* by Arthur Knight – and some gym clothes and a pair of smelly sneakers and a large metal film canister.

The octagon-shaped film cannister measured approximately 17" x 16" x 3". A handle on top, it was the kind you saw projectionists hauling into booths at movie houses in the days before digital technology.

The cannister was locked. She shook it. There was a muffled sound, like paper shifting about inside. A sticker on the side read "Rodacor 2/5 35mm." A tag identified the film as the second reel of *The Color of Money*, Paul Newman's sequel to *The Hustler* ... if indeed there was a 35mm film inside the can. It didn't feel heavy enough for 2,000 feet of celluloid film.

Hmm, interesting, Aggie thought as she shut the locker door and twirled the dial to relock it.

CHAPTER THIRTEEN

On the Ground News

Chief Jim Purdue was rankled that a slick lawyer had come waltzing into the station with a Writ from Judge Bristol to release his prisoner. The more he thought about it, the angrier he got. He remembered the lawyer – a Burpyville ambulance chaser named J. Harold Wentworth who had defended that guy who killed the previous police chief. Word on the street had it that Johnny Wentworth was about to be disbarred for dipping into escrow accounts. A crook defending crooks.

Wentworth had pulled a few strings with the judge. How did he do that?

Everything became clearer when Mayor Tidemore – himself a former attorney – explained that Judge John Lawrence Bristol was this guy Wentworth's uncle. The judge's wife was a Yager, just like Johnny Wentworth's mother. (That's why Judge Bristol had been forced to recuse himself in the recent murder trial of Henry "Hank" Yager, the family connection.)

That made the Writ of Habeas Corpus all the more fishy. But it was within the province of a judge to issue one if he saw fit. A Get-Out-of-Jail-Free card for Robert Di Nero – or whatever his name was.

~ ~ ~

"I'm driving up first thing in the morning," confirmed Lucius Plancus to the WZUR station manager. "I'll have something on that murder for tomorrow's five o'clock news."

The radio station's two most listened-to programs were the 6 a.m. and 5 p.m. news. Drive-times – that's when most people listened to the radio, trapped in their cars on the way to and from work.

Calling the programs "On the Ground News" had been a stroke of genius, Plancus thought. Yes, it had been *his* idea. On the Ground implied "on the spot," "up close," "at the scene." The name had been chosen to deliberately position them against a TV station over to the east that had a news helicopter – Eye in the Sky, they promoted it. Something a small radio station could never afford. So why not turn a negative into a positive!

"Keep in touch," said the station manager, giving Plancus a vague wave. Quite frankly he'd be glad to have this carping giant out of his hair for a few days. Too bad if Kenny Kincaid didn't like being recalled.

Plancus's trip would have been canceled if the station manager knew the perp had already been released from jail. Kenny had heard about it, but didn't tell his boss – irked at being pulled off the story. The Jolly Red Giant had struck again, but Kenny would get a measure of revenge seeing the big man sent off on a wild goose chase. Sources had it that the alleged killer – that actor who called himself Robert Di Nero – was already back in Indy where he lived.

"Don't worry, I'll get you the inside story on that mad dog killer," Lucius Plancus was boasting as he left the station. "Put Kenny to reading the weather report, something he's better suited for."

"Look, Lucius, the weather's important too," insisted the station manager. "What about all those people getting killed by that tornado this week? That's a big story."

"When a twister hits the WZUR radio antenna, call me."

"Aw, c'mon. No tornados are gonna touch down in this part of Indiana. Never have, never will. You can bet a week's salary on that."

He would have lost.

PART II

"The north and south winds met where the house stood, and made it the exact center of the cyclone. In the middle of a cyclone the air is generally still, but the great pressure of the wind on every side of the house raised it up higher and higher, until it was at the very top of the cyclone; and there it remained and was carried miles and miles away as easily as you could carry a feather."

- L. Frank Baum,
The Wonderful Wizard of Oz

CHAPTER FOURTEEN

The Tornado

Indiana lies on the edge of Tornado Alley, that swath of the Midwest known for the propensity for tornados touching down. No need to argue that Florida has more twisters per 10,000 square miles than any other state – 12.2 on the average. If you've ever been through a tornado, these statistics don't matter. The fact that Indiana ranks number 16 among those states -- with 6.1 on the average – is enough to make you think about building a storm cellar.

The most extreme tornado in recorded history was 1925's Tri-State Tornado, a massive twister that spread through Missouri, Illinois, and Indiana. It holds the record for the longest path (219 miles), longest duration (3 ½ hours), and fastest forward speed (73 MPH). Also it was the deadliest tornado in US history (695 fatalities all told – 71 in Indiana).

Then came the 1965 Palm Sunday tornado outbreak, which saw 47 tornados (32 significant, 17 violent, 21 killers). This was the deadliest tornado outbreak in Indiana history, with 137 people killed and 1,200 injured.

The intensity of tornados is measured by the Enhanced Fujita Scale. The EF Scale ranks storms from 0 to 5, based on the damage they cause, not wind speed. The scale offers only a proximity of wind speeds ranging from about 65 MPH at EF0 to over 200 MPH at EF5.

Tornados have been recorded on all continents except Antarctica. However, the US has more than any other country, averaging 1,274 tornados per year as opposed to Canada's 100.

While most tornados occur in the spring, they can happen year-round. Due to temperatures, they typically take place in the late afternoon between 3 and 7 p.m.

That's why nobody was expecting an EF3 tornado to hit Caruthers Corners in northeastern Indiana at 7:43 a.m. on a chilly day in November. It was meteorologically unlikely.

~ ~ ~

That morning Aggie ran the two blocks to her Grammy and Grampy's house, Tige barking at her heels. She'd left her algebra textbook there last night, and this side trip to retrieve it may have saved her life.

"There's your school book," Maddy pointed to the coffee table in the den. "Right where you left it. Now get to school."

"Thanks, Grammy."

"Want some watermelon cookies for a lunch snack? I just took a batch out of the oven." She often did her baking in the early morning when it was cooler.

"Yes, please."

"Hurry it up. You're already late."

"I know." Aggie was hurriedly dumping a handful of cookies into a Ziploc bag when she heard the siren. "What's that? A fire?"

Maddy paused to listen. "No, I think that's the tornado warning." The fire department had a special siren for approaching landspouts. But Maddy couldn't remember the last time she'd heard it.

Just then, the phone rang. "Yes?" Maddy answered.

"Is Aggie with you?" It was her father, Maddy's son-in-law.

"She's right here."

"Thank goodness. Get everybody down in the cellar quick as you can. A twister's heading our way."

"What about Tilly and the girls?"

"They're on their way over here to the Town Hall. We'll hold up in the basement." Luckily, the Taylor house where Mark and Tilly lived was only a block from the big red-brick Town Hall building. As was his habit, Mayor Mark Tidemore was already at work. He always arrived early to have his "quiet time," when he could get things done without interruption. His work day was one of constant interruptions – councilmen dropping in, the tax assessor knocking on his door, local citizens registering complaints, phone calls from friends and relatives and supporters.

Maddy slammed the phone down, shouting, "Beau, come downstairs – hurry!"

"What is it, Grammy?" asked her granddaughter.

"A twister. You and Tige get down in the cellar quick as you can. And take those cookies with you."

"Okay," the girl said, scooping all the cookies off the baking tin and into the largest Ziploc bag at hand. "C'mon, Tige. We gotta take shelter."

"What is it?" called Beau Madison, hobbling down the stairs, buttoning his flannel shirt. His face was strained, recognizing the urgency in his wife's voice.

"Mark just called. A twister's headed this way."

"The cellar," he said. Moving faster. "I heard the siren but I thought it must be a test or something. I don't think I've heard it go off in a good ten years or more."

"I want to call Freddie, make sure his family is safe."

"No need. Our son is the fire chief. He's probably the one who called Mark."

Maddy padded down the cellar steps to join Aggie and her dog, while Beau slammed home the bolt to the thick door. The siren was still wailing, but another sound took over – a rumbling sound like an approaching locomotive. But there was no train in Caruthers Corners.

"Hunker down over there in that corner," ordered Beau Madison. "That section has been reinforced. We should be safe there."

Then the lights went out.

~ ~ ~

The house shook. Jars and cans fell off the shelves in the storm cellar. The roar of the tornado so loud Beau couldn't hear his wife's shouts. He could feel the pressure drop. His eardrums felt like they were about to pop. It was very dark there in the cellar under the house.

Less than three minutes later it was over.

"Are you okay?" called Beau.

"I'm fine," said Maddy breathlessly. "Just a little shook up."

"Tige and I are all right," answered his granddaughter. But it was obvious she'd been crying.

Beau was relieved. "Good, good," he said. "Everybody's safe."

"Is it over?" sniffled Aggie.

"Yep. The twister passed right over us," replied Beau. "No telling where it is now. Sometimes they keep on going. Other times they blow out."

"Can we get out of this storm cellar?" suggested Maddy. "I want to see if we have any house left."

"Hang on, there's a flashlight somewhere in this supply box over here." There was a rustling sound, then a click and a yellow beam of light bounced off the sagging ceiling.

"Wow. Look at that," said Aggie. "The roof nearly fell in."

"We better get out of here before it does," said her grandfather. He pointed the light toward the cellar stairs. They were still intact, although slightly crooked. "Follow me, but be careful. There may be all kinds of debris up there. Boards with nails. Broken glass. Unstable walls. Dangerous stuff."

They climbed the stairs cautiously, one foot, then the other. Beau unsnapped the lock, but the door refused to open. Its frame was warped. "Hold on. Let me put my shoulder to it."

The thin man put his 160 pounds against the wooden door, but all it did was groan. Nothing budged.

"Let me help," said Maddy, adding her 140 pounds to the task.

Quilt Block

Plop! – the door unceremoniously flew open.

The sight that greeted them reminded Maddy of a surreal painting by René Magritte. Staring through the doorframe she could see blue sky. But there was no house on the other side of the door.

CHAPTER FIFTEEN

Damage Report

About two-thirds of Caruthers Corners was missing. Grand three-story homes and brick storefront buildings, mighty oak trees and telephone poles, garish billboards and doublewide house trailers on the edge of town – all swept away by an angry god wielding a cosmic broom.

The Madisons' fine old Victorian home was gone, as if it had been carried somewhere over the rainbow to land on the Wicked Witch of the East. Only the tiled kitchen floor and a scattering of broken pipes pointing skyward signified that a structure had ever been there. Not a wall or window or single stick of furniture was left on the site where the house had once stood.

Maddy paused on the sidewalk, mouth agape, looking around in wonderment. The landscape of their neighborhood was so changed as to be unrecognizable. Beau simply shook his head wearily, knowing that hard times were ahead – for the Madison family and for the town.

"Gee, where's your house, Grampy?" asked Aggie, eyes wide.

"That's a good question," Beau answered. "Sitting in the next county would be my guess."

"Oh my," said Maddy. At a loss for words.

The entire length of Melon Pickers Row had been obliterated. Houses missing or ripped in half by the 150

MPH winds. But only one block over, the pristine rows of houses were totally untouched.

"Let's hike over to the Town Hall and check on your mom and dad and sisters," Beau suggested to Aggie. "But be careful where you step."

"Okay."

The trio began their trek. The wreckage left behind by the tornado blocked the street in some places. A red Kia was wedged in the Y-fork of a large, leafless tree. A misplaced house sat smack-dab in the middle of Fourth Avenue. Two right-hand-drive mail trucks were "parked" on the flat roof of the US Post Office. A dinette table with cereal bowls in place was found on the sidewalk of North Main Street as if awaiting someone to sit down for breakfast. It was a scene of pandemonium: shredded homes, downed power lines, and streets littered with tossed cars.

From several blocks away they could see the red-brick façade of the Town Hall, still standing defiantly, like the flag in the "Star Spangled Banner." But further down Main Street the storefront that had once housed Ace Hardware and Pic A Pair Shoes had been replaced by a vacant lot.

The cinderblock building occupied by the police department was still solidly in place, as was the stainless-steel structure of Cozy Café. However, the Dairy Queen with its soft ice cream machines and hot dog grills had somehow vaporized.

Looking across the Town Square, Aggie was surprised that the ancient 16-gondola Ferris wheel had totally disappeared, like one of those grandiose magic tricks by David Copperfield. Now you see it, now you don't.

The spire of Peaceful Meadows, the 110-year-old Baptist church, was tilted to one side, like a broken twig. The roof of the Troxler house was totally missing, but the house next door only had a few shingles loosened. Most of the trees in the Town Square had been uprooted. All the bronze statues of Town Founders were tipped over like dead soldiers.

But even more disturbing: The big blue Victorian mansion that Aggie called home had been leveled, leaving only piles of rubble behind on the narrow lot facing the park. The historic Taylor house – along with Aggie's bedroom, her closet full of new school clothes, her treasured American Doll collection, and Tige's dog bowl – was no more.

How strange.

Agnes Millicent Tidemore was homeless.

~ ~ ~

Maddy and Beau were homeless too. The heartbreaking fact wasn't the loss of the beloved house where they had raised their children – Bill , Tilly, and Freddy – but the loss of all their personal effects: The baby books, the high school trophies, the vacation souvenirs, the Christmas presents, the family photographs. These could never be replaced.

They paused on the steps of the Town Hall, looking out at the low skyline, inspecting the devastation. A path of destruction led from the Industrial Park all the way to the E-Z Seat chair factory, a gash that zigzagged along Main Street and across the Town Square before barreling its way up Melon Pickers Row – taking the Madisons' big Victorian home with it.

The alarm at the fire station was silent now. But the distant shriek of a siren announced a paramedic truck heading to Burpyville Memorial with a load of injured survivors. That was a good sign. Paramedics indicated the fire department had withstood the tornado. Maybe their son Freddie was safe.

Banging on the wide front door of the Town Hall got the attention of Jasper Beanie, the building's custodian. "Oh, Mr. Madison, it's you and the Missus. And Miss Aggie too. I'm sure the Mayor's gonna be relieved to see you."

The trio shuffled into the great hall in the center of the building. Refugees of the storm. "Where is everybody?"

"Most are still in the basement. You know, down there where the public records are kept. It's as safe as a cyclone cellar. Dug into solid bedrock. But that big landspout spared this building, thank goodness."

"My daddy's down there?" asked Aggie.

"No, little missy. Your daddy's up in the conference room on the next floor, trying to get through to the governor. To have him to declare this town a Disaster Area. But all the phone lines are down."

"That doesn't surprise me," nodded Beau. "Electricity seems to be out too!"

"Go on up," said Jasper Beanie. The town drunk, he looked amazingly sober at this particular moment. "I'm sure Mayor Tidemore will want to know his daughter's safe."

"Thank, Jasper."

Beau led his wife and granddaughter up the steep wooden stairwell to the second floor where they found Mark Tidemore huddled with Police Chief Jim Purdue. Jim was on his police radio, patched into the Governor's office in Indy through his PD counterpart in nearby Burpyville. Apparently, Caruthers Corners was the only municipality struck by the EF3 tornado. This was definitely the town's worst disaster since the Great Fire of 1899.

~ ~ ~

In the United States, hurricanes and tropical storms are the only kinds of weather events that get a name: Wilma, Katrina, Harvey. Other major storms such as tornados remain unnamed – at best referred to by location and year. Since 2012, more than 60 nameless weather disasters have caused more than $41 billion in damages.

This event would be referred to as the "2018 Northeastern Indiana Tornado."

~ ~ ~

"Daddy," shouted Aggie, running into her father's arms. "You're all right!"

"Yes, dumpling. This old Town Hall building is solid as a rock. And it has a good basement. Lots of people are safe down there – including your mother and sisters."

"Your Aunt Bootsie's down there too," added Chief Purdue as he got off the radio.

The mayor turned to his police chief. "What did the Governor's office say?"

"Said he's mobilizing National Guard units. And notifying FEMA's National Response Coordination

Center. Help's on the way. We should see Guardsmen by this afternoon."

"Good, good."

Just then, the conference room door swung open and in walked Deputy Pete Hitzer with Deputy Tommy Truehart a few steps behind him. The Chief had sent them out to reconnoiter the town. "It's a mess!" reported Petie without any preamble. "That twister cut a path right through the middle of town. Lots of buildings gone. Probably a lot of folks dead. Not everybody had a storm cellar."

"Yeah," repeated Deputy Truehart, "a mess."

Petie Hitzer ducked his head, police cap in his hands. "Sorry about your house, Mr. and Mrs. Madison. Yours too, Mayor."

"Hardly anything left standing," acknowledged Beau. "But we were safe down there in our storm cellar."

"Thanks for taking care of Aggie," said the Mayor, putting a hand on his father-in-law's shoulder.

"You bet. Is the rest of your family okay?"

"Thankfully, yes. Everybody's down in the basement. They're staying put till we're sure there are no more landspouts roaming around out there." Sometimes tornadoes traveled in packs.

"Did you check on Cookie and Ben?" Maddy asked the deputies.

"They're just fine," said Petie. "The twister missed their farmhouse. Didn't hit that side of town. Haney Bros. Zoo and Exotic Animal Refuge came through okay too. Happy the elephant was a little upset, but Bombay Martinez is calming her down."

"Bombay's good with the animals," said Aggie. Patting her dog Tige reassuringly on the head as she spoke.

"And Edgar and Lizzie?" asked Beau. Edgar Ridenour was his weekend fishing buddy.

"The twister didn't go near the river," Tommy told them. The Ridenours lived on the banks of the Wabash. "I took a ride out that way. Everything looked pretty normal. No trees down or anything."

Petie added, "Your house is still standing, Chief. I did a drive-by. The dairy farm next door's okay too. All the cows safe."

"That's good news. But I'm still glad we took shelter here. We're one of the few houses without a storm shelter, so things could have been dicey if that twister had zigged instead of zagged."

"E-Z Seat's gonna be out of business for a while. Half of the factory's missing," said Tommy. "But both of those big stone buildings on the hill – Miss Hoople's mansion and the Perricock Museum – escaped without a scratch. Looks like the hill protected them."

"Those big stone buildings are like fortresses," observed Maddy. "I think they will survive the Apocalypse."

"Thank goodness the twister missed the elementary school and the high school," said the Mayor. He'd had an earlier report. The students were already in school, due to starting time of 7:20 a.m. this year. That meant most of the kids in town were safe.

Chief Purdue added, "One school bus got toppled over but the driver came through with only a few bruises. He'd already let off his kids and was on his way home."

"How about Freddie and his family?" Maddy wanted to know.

"Freddie's family is downstairs," Jim Purdue told her. "He's over at the station directing his firemen. We're in touch by police radio."

"Freddie reports that the twister missed the station, so his men are ferrying injured people to the Burpyville hospital," said Mark Tidemore. "Local doctors are treating people too. Yost & Yost funeral home is collecting dead bodies, but they don't have much room."

"Any idea how many are dead?" asked Beau.

"No firm figures. Dozens, I think. Fatty Johnson got caught in his truck on South Main. Apparently, Maisie Daniels had a heart attack during the storm. Personally Yours Flowers & Gifts was totally destroyed – unfortunately with Oliver Micherson and Jeff Brown inside."

"Oh my," said Maddy. "Jeff Brown is Cookie's brother-in-law by her first husband."

"Others we know to be dead – Big Nose Evans, Elsie Warton, one of Abram Wagler's kids, that cranky old foreign guy Ivor Yokovich, and a cousin of Sad Sammy Hankins. Many more are reported missing. Freddie's firemen are doing search and rescue. He radios in as they identify the dead."

"Big Nose," said Beau. "He was serving his first term on the Town Council."

"Bob Norris Evans was an irascible cuss," nodded Mark. "But he loved this town. He'll be a great loss."

"Any word on my sister Maisie?" asked Maddy. Maisie Walters, her "long lost" twin sister, owned Cozy Café, the stainless-steel diner on South Main.

Mark shook his head. "Not yet. But the diner's still standing."

"The police station was spared too," said Chief Purdue. "Myrtle Dobbler's over there coordinating all the emergency channels. Phone lines are down but we have radio communication with key service providers."

"Dollar General's okay too. Lost a plate glass window, but nothing serious," said Deputy Truehart. Tommy had worked there before being hired to the police department.

"How about Don?" Donald Smyth was the general manager of the cut-rate emporium. A likeable, obsequious man, he was fairly new to town. Transferred in from Terre Haute only last year.

"Don was at home, hiding in the cellar with his wife."

"Good for him."

"Heirlooms Unlimited got wiped out," Petie Hitzer noted. "The entire building and all its antiques are completely gone. There's just a foundation left."

"What about Fat Karl?" Three-hundred-fifty-pound Karl Schaeffer was manager of the antiques outlet. Karl was so corpulent he could barely get down the aisles of the crowded shop.

"Fat Karl's okay," said Petie. "He hadn't left for work yet. And the tornado never came near his home way up there at Never Ending Swamp."

"Errol Baumgartner's injured pretty bad," reported Tommy Truehart. "They think he might not make it. The paramedics carried him down to Burpyville Memorial."

Chief Purdue looked up. "Errol? He lives up near Never Ending Swamp too. I thought you boys said the tornado didn't get up that way."

"It didn't," Tommy explained. "Errol had come to town early to pick up some feed from Grumman's Granary. Got caught in his truck. The pickup wound up smashed against a wall on Rocking Chair Lane. Broke his hip and crushed his ribs."

"That's bad."

"I'll say," Tommy nodded. "That was a brand-new truck. A 2018 baby-blue Ford F-150 XLT Supercrew – a sweet ride!"

"I was talking about Errol," said the police chief.

"Yeah, him too," said the deputy.

CHAPTER SIXTEEN

Eyewitness Accounts

Lucius Plancus drove up to Caruthers Corners that morning to take over the big murder story. He'd enjoyed the ride, the top down on his '94 Oldsmobile Cutlass Supreme, an ancient powerhouse with a 6-cylinder 3.4 liter 24-valve dual overhead camshaft engine. The black leather interior was as soft as a baby's skin.

The sky was dark up that way. Probably a thunderstorm. He might have to stop and put the top up.

He was feeling pretty good today. His colleague Kenny Kincaid had been called back to WZUR to do the weather. Reading National Weather Service reports off the computer screen – bo-o-ring! Served Kenny right, the incompetent doofus.

Lucius Plancus didn't know it but this trip would gift him with the biggest story of his career ... and Kincaid would miss out on the weather story of the century ... well, local weather story ... when the EF3 tornado hit the town at 7:43 a.m.

He arrived there at 9:15. It looked like a bomb had dropped.

But Plancus was a pro. He wasted no time getting on the air with a live broadcast.

"Lucius Plancus here for On the Ground News. I'm standing at Ground Zero for the

devastating tornado that hit Caruthers Corners, a small town in northeaster Indiana, this morning. Surrounding me is chaos and destruction, homes destroyed and business laid waste. Many people are dead. I'm talking to survivors of the twister, interviews you will only hear on WZUR ..."

The interviewees included:

Tim Mischler, 42, said he had been at his parents' mobile home when the tornado struck. The three were awakened by the wind, which picked up the home and moved it halfway into the neighbor's yard, shattering glass and shaking the home.

He and his parents escaped unharmed, but they heard several of their neighbors calling for help. A nearby mobile home was overturned, he said, and another appeared to have been obliterated.

"All you could hear was people screaming, 'Help me! Help me!'" Tim recalled. "You could see them. There was people under walls, people half-naked with just sheets on, bleeding. It was terrifying. A whole wall of a trailer was on a lady. There was really nothing we could do."

The tornado smashed 12 trailers in the Happy Times Mobile Home Park. It held only 14. A dozen residents were injured, but thankfully no one died.

"It wouldn't be a tornado without house trailers," remarked park manager Hans Bitner. "Twisters seem to seek 'em out like magnets. This is the worst one I've ever seen. Happy Times is plum wiped out." He would declare bankruptcy later that week.

~ ~ ~

"The whole neighborhood's gone. The wall of my fireplace is all that is left of my house," observed Michael Allen Palley, a 47-year-old accountant. "My neighborhood was wiped out in a matter of seconds."

"All I could see was debris," said 50-year-old Gabe Hilty. "I thought it was a bad dream." Gabe Hilty was the town barber. Snippets Inc. had been reduced to a pile of bricks.

"It completely flattened some of the neighbor-hoods here in town, hundreds of homes. I've never seen anything like this, and I hope I never see it again," Mary Hegler said. Miss Hegler, 58, was the local librarian. The library was completely destroyed, all of its books taking to the wind like butterflies.

~ ~ ~

"I was taking out the trash when the sirens came on," said Donny Kensinger, a 7th grader at Caruthers Elementary. He'd been home with a cold. "Luckily there was a siren extremely close to where I lived."

"I think the scariest part was when the funnel cloud passed over and you could literally feel the air pressure change and hear the house creaking," added Donny's father. Ed Kensinger, 38, was the manager at Food Lion.

"The sound was deafening," remembered Ed McGonigal, a neighbor two houses over. "You could not hear a darn thing other than the tornado and the wood splintering and breaking. I also could not see anything. The darkness was insane. The first shake of the house split something and I saw a brief amount of light and that went away almost immediately. Being inside of it was like being thrown like a rag doll. I remember hitting the pavement outside of our house on the ground and continuing inside tons of debris from our house and the darn thing ripping my iPhone from my hand, then I blacked out."

"There was lots of popping in the beginning," said 15-year-old high-school student Joanie McPhee. "I remember hearing the glass shatter and the debris even began to squeeze through the cracks of the door. The sound was loud and pretty scary. I don't know if I'd compare it to a train, but it's kind of hazy in my memory. I remember my ears popping more. A sleeper would almost certainly wake. Not only is the tornado loud, but the rattling of the building is unignorable."

"It is surreal to be able to recognize the sound of the house you have built your life in for the past seven years ripping apart by a natural force," recounted Joanie's father, 38-year-old Benjamin McPhee. "It is insane because in my mind I could very clearly make out the large crash of our vehicle (although I didn't know it was a vehicle, just something big) crashing through the wall into my room. I could hear electronics popping and transformers blowing. I could hear the roof peeling away from our house. The thing that amazed me is that I could hear all of this as clear as day while the tornado blew over. Hearing everything separate, but also together."

~ ~ ~

John Powers Petrovitch was a professional storm chaser who'd been featured on the Weather Channel.

Even with 35 years' experience in chasing tornados, he wasn't prepared for what he witnessed this morning. Coming up behind the storm, he saw the funnel cloud touch down near the Caruthers Corners Industrial Park. His truck narrowly survived this brush with the twister.

As Petrovitch described it: "When this thing came down, it was about a hundred yards wide. I saw rotating rain curtains like a robo-carwash, just real fast rain curtains spinning on the ground. I mean as soon as it hit the first building or whatever it hit first on the southwest side of the city, it instantly turned black for about ten seconds, and then it went from that to about a quarter mile wide in a matter of seconds. When it was a quarter mile wide I was a good half-mile south of it, so I was fine. I wasn't in the vortex. As we kept coming east on 10th Street, it just got wider and wider and wider, and it literally tried to suck me into the south wall of the tornado. I saw a car in front of me get picked up and hurdled into a field just west of me. At that point, it blew out my windows. I got cut up. Glass was all inside of my Chevy Avalanche, and I had to abort the mission. I had glass all over me, so I turned the rear end of the car into the wind, because it was about 120 MPH behind me. Debris was everywhere. In the sky there were millions of pieces of debris flying over me, by me, near me. Just everywhere."

~ ~ ~

"The feeling of community about the town was insane," said Pricilla Moretz, a 15-year-old sophomore at Caruthers High. "For a short while, everyone was family. You saw someone and you offered everything you had to help. My father went out to our neighbors' house and helped them out of their basement because their house was flattened where ours still had quite a few walls standing. He literally gave that man the shirt he was wearing because our neighbor wasn't wearing one, and his blew away."

"My neighbor saved my life," attested Jerry Peach, 47, an employee at ZapData. "A tree fell on me, but he pulled me out. Otherwise, I'd still be there."

"A terrifying experience," said Fritz Berber, 62, a local mailman. "Hope I never go through one of these again. I've only got a few more years till retirement. I'd like to live to see it."

CHAPTER SEVENTEEN

Crimestopper Tip

The tornado having passed, Lizzie Ridenour backed her Mercedes-Benz out of the garage and drove over to the Hoople Quilting Heritage Museum. As its executive director, she needed to make sure it hadn't suffered any storm damage.

Fortunately, the little quilting museum lay outside the twister's path. The building looked just as pristine as she'd left it last night. When closing up to head home, she'd been extra careful in locking the front doors. Next Monday was the opening of the new Marie Webster exhibit and the prized 1925 quilt – "Pink Dogwoods in Appliqué" – was already hanging there in the main gallery. A large room with a vaulted ceiling, this gallery was the latest addition to the facility.

That's why Lizzie's heart nearly stopped when she saw that the museum's front doors were standing wide open.

Had the doors been blown open by the storm? Maybe. But none of the other buildings in the neighborhood looked touched by this morning's tornado.

Parking in front, she ran up the steps and examined the doors. The lock looked twisted, as if the door had been pried open with a crowbar. Would a storm do damage like that? It seemed unlikely.

Hurrying inside, she headed straight for the big gallery. But as she entered the room, she stopped dead in her tracks. Staring up at the wall, her worst fear was confirmed: The "Pink Dogwoods in Appliqué" quilt was gone.

~ ~ ~

Aggie was worried about Bobby Elwood until a deputy confirmed that Bobby's family had survived the tornado, their house intact.

James Elwood – Bobby's dad – worked at Home Depot, which didn't see any damage at the main store. The funnel cloud had touched down two miles to the east, taking out much of the Caruthers Corners Industrial Park. ZapData had been completely wiped out. And Home Depot's auxiliary warehouse was gone too. Even the nearby water towel had been blown over like a collapsed Erector Set.

The Elwood home was located near the animal shelter. First thing after the twister passed through, Bobby raced over to the complex of buildings to check on the dogs, cats, and one lone iguana. All had been fine, other than the dogs being a little frightened. The sound made by that tornado was like standing next to the engine of a 747. Enough to scare man or beast!

Bobby worked part-time at the animal shelter. Feeding these rescued animals took a lot of Kibble. But his availability was limited now that he had a girlfriend. He often hung out after school with Aggie, barely able to squeeze out the extra hours to walk dogs and pet cats and go by the flower shop to pick up food for the iguana, Ol' Horace. This awesome 4-foot-long reptile doted on hibiscus and other blossoms. Personally

Yours donated unsold flowers, but what would the shelter do now that the flower shop had been blown away by the deadly twister?

~ ~ ~

Taking time off work, Bobby's dad was helping with the search and rescue. Jim Elwood rode along with one of the paramedics, a chubby pre-med student named Sven Oberly. Sven was getting grad credits for his work driving an ambulance. Sort of like being an ER doc-on-the-go.

Jim Elwood had noticed something odd just after the tornado plowed through town. He and his partner had made a run over to the Industrial Park to pick up the new night watchman, the guy who replaced Matea Davis. Still on duty at 7:43 a.m., Fritz Bruckhalter had been injured by flying debris. A broken clavicle. A few inches higher and the brick would have beaned him in the head, possibly fatal. Crawling into a metal drainage pipe probably saved his life.

As Jim and Sven drove past the new quilting museum, they noticed a figure at the front door, bashing at it with a crowbar. A looter? Maybe so, but Fritz Bruckhalter was in a lot of pain. The dispatcher at the police department told them to take Bruckhalter directly to Doc Medford's office. Doc was treating patients as fast as he could, almost like an assembly line. Fritz Bruckhalter couldn't wait.

Later that morning Jim mentioned the possible looter to the Fire Chief and Freddie passed along the Crimestopper Tip to Police Chief Purdue. Jim Purdue had asked Myrtle to send the new deputy over to take a look. By the time Deputy Truehart got there, Lizzie had already discovered the robbery. So Tommy Truehart made a note to file a report, then moved on to the next emergency. Somebody had spotted a body in a tree. He got so busy that he forgot to write up the incident report.

CHAPTER EIGHTEEN

Coming Out

People were starting to venture out of their homes to survey the damage. Like the proverbial groundhog coming out of his hole to see his shadow. The scene was disturbing to local residents. It looked as if the town had been ripped in half, east and west sides remaining untouched while the twister slashed up the middle.

Most houses had storm cellars. Rarely used, they were like having an insurance policy you hoped to never collect on. The croaky old siren at the fire station had provided adequate warning and homeowners had taken to their cellars like burrowing animals running from an approaching predator.

Now they climbed out, blinking in the sunlight, studying the bright blue sky. No storm clouds in sight. Yet only an hour ago the sun had blinked out, a few seconds of total darkness like a solar eclipse.

"You okay?" one neighbor called to the other.

"Yeah, how 'bout you?"

"I'm in better shape than my house."

Some had only a downed tree or a missing chimney to show for the storm. Others had lost entire three-story houses. You could almost measure the edge of the twister down to the inch, yards where green perennial ryegrass suddenly gave way to bare ground where grass had been plucked blade-by-blade by the swirling winds.

~ ~ ~

Myrtle Dobbler's sister Elvina came down to the police station to relieve her. The two traded off hours on no discernable schedule. Chief Purdue was never sure who was on duty, but it didn't matter: The two women were as interchangeable as GE lightbulbs.

They looked enough alike to be twins, although there was actually a two-year gap in their ages. Nobody could remember which was older. Their frizzy black hair surrounded oval faces, the mocha skin fresh and shining as if well-scrubbed. Both were short, plump ladies – the result of sedimentary sit-down jobs and poor eating habits. They lived out of vending machines, a diet of Pepsis and potato chips and Ring Dings.

"You okay?" said Elvina as she slid into the padded office chair in front of the police radio and scanner equipment. With all the knobs and dials it looked like she was preparing to pilot a spaceship.

"You bet, sis. This building is solid concrete. Like a bomb shelter. The blocks are reinforced by steel pillars. Couldn't knock it down with a bulldozer." The tornado had passed right over the police department with little more damage than a bent radio antenna.

"I was worried about you, caught here in the middle of the storm."

"Gave me pause when the lights went out and the emergency generator kicked in," admitted Myrtle. She picked up her handbag, ready to go home and catch a few hours sleep. After that, the sisters would swap off again. Both single, they shared a rental on Sixth Avenue.

"Our house is still standing," reported Elvina. "That funnel cloud was two or three streets over."

"That's good news. I was worried the house would be sitting in the next county. That would be a hard commute."

~ ~ ~

Bootsie slunk up from the Town Hall's basement. She was getting claustrophobic down there. Besides that, Tilly Tidemore's three youngest children were driving her batty. And Freddie Madison's little daughter was none better. Probably a good thing that she and Jim never had any children. She couldn't stand the little buggers. Dog were much easier to contend with than kids. The Purdues now had three pups.

She found her husband on the second floor, ensconced in the conference room with the Mayor and Beau and Maddy. Aggie and her fuzzy little mutt were there too. Aggie was not in the same irritating category as her younger siblings. At fifteen, she was nearly grown.

Aggie would have agreed on both points.

"Bootsie, honey," the police chief greeted her. "You should stay down there with the others till we're sure this thing is over. That twister might circle back."

"It's perfectly safe to come out," she argued. "Look out the window. It's quit raining and the sky is blue." Everybody in the Midwest was familiar with the Blue Sky Rule: When you can see a blue sky, the tornado has passed, because skies are always blue on the backside of a storm.

"Okay, okay. I'm just being overly cautious, I suppose. But a lot of people who we know are dead out there,"

"Cookie? Lizzie?"

"Both are okay," interjected Maddy. "Petie and Tommy checked on them."

"Oh, thank goodness."

"Did someone mention my name?" said Lizzie Ridenour, appearing at the conference room door.

"Lizzie, what are you doing here?" said Chief Jim Purdue.

"I want to report a robbery."

CHAPTER NINETEEN

History of Twisters

Cookie Bentley couldn't believe the devastation she saw as she drove into town. There on her left was Fifth Avenue, all nice and normal. Then came Fourth Avenue, a scene of total pandemonium. The Post Office with two mail trucks sitting on its roof. Houses reduced to Pik-Up-Stix. A refrigerator on the sidewalk. A vacant lot where a dry cleaner had once been. Beyond it, Melon Pickers Row looked as if a giant broom had swept all the beautiful Victorian homes away. Maddy's house was missing, as if it had been erased from the picture. Then came Third Avenue, with everything back to normal, no damaged buildings.

Weird, the way the familiar landscape had been rearranged into an unfamiliar panorama. It looked like a giant canvas depicting Hieronymus Bosch's vision of Hades.

Cookie wanted to cry.

~ ~ ~

Ben Bentley walked over to Haney Bros. Zoo and Exotic Animals Refuge to check on the elephant and baboon and tiger – in all more than a dozen "guests," as they referred to the resident fauna. Unlike typical zoos that put animals on display in cages for the public's entertainment, this facility had morphed into an open-air sanctuary for circus animals in need of a

105

home. Kids could interact with the animals, pet them (well, not the tiger), see them up close.

Bombay Martinez, A/K/A Juan Martinez, had everything under control. Happy the elephant was still jittery. Sneezy the baboon was nervously following Bombay around the grounds. Bashful the tiger was in hiding. And a couple of the new coyotes were yip-yip-yipping. The other animal were acting fairly normal.

"All's good here," Bombay assured him. "Other than three rhesus monkeys escaping during the chaos. But they'll turn up when they get hungry. There ain't no banana trees 'round here. Them rascals are used to getting room service."

"How close did the tornado come to the zoo?"

"Not too close, but I could see the funnel cloud from here," Bombay said. "It touched down over that way." He pointed toward the Industrial Park. About 80% of all tornados come from the West or Southwest. That was pretty much the direction that the zookeeper indicated.

Ben stared into the distance. "Looks like the water tower is down. That means nobody will have water."

"What about our animals?"

"They'll be fine. We have our own well. And a gasoline-powered generator to pump it."

Bombay pointed again. "The spout disappeared over that way. Somewhere near the chair factory. It was moving away from us. Cutting through town."

"Cookie's on her way into town to check out the damage, see if our friends are okay."

"Is that safe?"

"Yeah, that twister's blown itself out. Or gone on with the big storm. At any rate, it's done here."

"Has there ever been a tornado here before?" He'd come to the area four years ago with the circus.

"Not that I know of. My family has lived in these parts for over a hundred years, so I'd think I would have heard of it if we'd ever had one."

"You sure?"

"I'll ask Cookie. She's the historian."

~ ~ ~

Cookie was headed into town. But if she'd been there she would have told them that the earliest records of tornados in Indiana go back to 1814. However, little is known about those early twisters.

More recent records show the following death tolls from Hoosier State tornados:

- April 13, 1852 - New Harmony - 16 dead.
- May 14, 1886 - Anderson - 43 dead.
- March 23, 1913 - Terre Haute - 21 dead.
- March 23, 1917 - New Castle - 21 dead.
- March 28, 1920 - Allen through Wayne counties - 39 people killed by 3 tornados.
- April 17, 1922 - Warren through Delaware counties - 14 dead.
- March 18, 1925 - Tri-State tornado - 71 dead.
- March 26, 1948 - Vigo to Jay counties - 20 dead.
- May 11, 1949 - Sullivan and Clay counties - Coatsville destroyed - 14 dead.
- April 11, 1965 - Palm Sunday Outbreak - 11 tornados hit 20 counties - 137 dead.

- April 3, 1974 - Super Outbreak - 21 tornados hit 39 counties - 47 dead.
- March 10, 1986 - 8 tornados hit central and southern 9 counties - 1 dead, 48 injured.
- June 2, 1990 - 31 counties hit by 37 tornados, 8 dead - 220 injured.
- April 26, 1994 – Tippecanoe, Carroll – 3 dead.
- March 2, 2012 – Washington, Clark, Scott, Jefferson – 11 dead.

A 1989 publication from the U.S. Department of Commerce (National Weather Service) stated that between 1953 and 1980, Indiana averaged three deaths from eight tornados annually.

Between 1950 and 2016 Indiana recorded 1,457 tornados that killed 330 people and injured 5,301 others caught in their paths. Moving the average to almost 4½ deaths per year.

However, Caruthers Corners, founded in 1829, had never experienced a tornado in its recorded history.

CHAPTER TWENTY

Help Arrives

At Mayor Mark Tidemore's request, the governor activated 150 National Guard troops to come to the community's aid.

A state public affairs officer affirmed, "We stand ready to assist in whatever manner the town may need to help them recover from this tragedy."

By that afternoon troops were on site – providing debris removal, patrolling streets to prevent looting, providing power to critical infrastructure, maintaining traffic control, distributing ice and water, and flying helicopters overhead to aid in the search and recovery efforts.

According to the National Guard Bureau (NGB), Indiana Guard members also were helping Emergency Medical Service personnel evacuate patients and deliver critically needed medication. "We were able to mobilize soldiers rapidly, and physically have them here within hours after this tragedy," said the spokesman.

The soldiers would work 12-hour shifts. A curfew from 7 p.m. to 7 a.m. was being enforced. Checkpoints stood at the main entrances to the town where drivers had to prove they lived in the town to enter. Other roads were blocked completely due to severe storm damage.

The Red Cross mobilized operations out of their Indianapolis Region. Three shelters were open by the end of day.

The Indianapolis Chamber of Commerce announced it would donate sugar, flour, meats, and potatoes to the tornado survivors.

Indiana Michigan Power was dispatching several teams to restore electricity.

Franklin Graham's Samaritan's Purse charity was sending food, water, and medicine.

Everybody was pitching in.

~ ~ ~

Cookie parked her Ford Explorer outside the boxy cement-block headquarters of the Caruthers Corners Police Department and barged through the front door. "Where is everybody?" she shouted to the dispatcher.

Elvina Dobbler looked up, surprised by the intrusion. "Oh, Cookie Bentley, you gave me a start. I almost jumped outta my skin." Like her sister, Elvina had a nut-brown complexion, but it looked intact.

"Maddy and Beau's house has blown away. Are they dead or missing?"

"No, ma'am. They're both down at the Town Hall. About everybody of consequence is down there. The Chief, his missus, the mayor and his family, Freddie Madison's family, li'l Aggie, the property clerk, the tax collector, dozens of other folks. And I heard over the po-lice radio that Mizz Ridenour just arrived. Everybody important's there but me and you."

~ ~ ~

By midday, Lucius Plancus was reporting that more than 30 people were estimated to be dead.

Indiana had not seen a disaster of this scale since the 1965 Palm Sunday tornados that killed 137 Hoosiers ... or more than 100 dead in the Great Flood of 1913 ... or the Hammond Circus Train Wreck of 1918 which resulted in the death of 86 performers ... or the 1925 Tri-State Tornado that saw 71 dead in Indiana.

The Tri-State Tornado had been estimated as an EF5, the highest end of the Enhanced Fujita Scale that measures damage caused by tornados. But that was just a guess. The original Fujita Scaled wasn't invented until 1971 by severe storms researcher Tetsuya "Ted" Fujita. And the enhanced version wasn't unveiled by the National Weather Service until 2006.

The current disaster was called an EF3, but some meteorologist argued that it should be classified as an EF4. The scale is based on damage, not wind speed.

CHAPTER TWENTY-ONE

No Second Sight

Matea Davis had been at his wigwam the night before the tornado struck, a lucky break for him. It was his get-away spot, this private camp in Injun Woods north of town. Since that tract of land was owned by the Sons of Anthony Wayne, as the Badger Patrol's new troop leader he had official permission to camp there. Sure, it was a long drive to work, but his rickety '98 Chevrolet Lumina made the trip without complaint, other than leaving a smoke-signal trail to mark its passage.

Had Matea been home, he might have been a casualty. His apartment on Fourth Avenue was completely destroyed by the 150 MPH cyclone winds. Matea's neighbor across the hall was swept away in his sleep, the body as yet unrecovered.

At age twenty-five, Matea was a handsome young Native American with high cheekbones and bronze skin and crow-black hair that hung nearly to his shoulders. A couple of years ago, he had come here to the land of his forbearers to get in touch with his tribal heritage. In the early 1800s his people had maintained a sizeable village along the Wabash. Today, Matea was the only known Potawatomi in this part of Indiana.

Growing up on the rez in Oklahoma, he had seen lots of tornados. He knew their dangerous and unpredictable nature. Oklahoma is the state with the third most tornados annually.

Matea remembered the 2013 El Reno Tornado that touched down over rural areas of Oklahoma. It was the widest tornado in recorded history, stretching across 2.6 miles at its peak. Measurements using mobile weather radar recorded winds in excess of 295 MPH within its vortex, the second-highest observed wind speeds on Earth. However, this twister didn't hit developed parts of the state, so its destruction was only rated as an EF3.

Indian lands suffered little damage from that one. Matea believed this was because tribal elders had performed an ancient ritual to turn the tornado away. After the ceremony, the El Reno tornado took an unexpected turn and veered away from the reservation's lands, a move not predicted by any of the NWS computer modeling of the funnel cloud's path.

Over the past 60 years Indian lands have seen less damage from tornados than have other portions of Oklahoma. Matea knew that various tribes in the red dirt state had enacted special ceremonies to warn away tornados. Kiowa women asked them for mercy. The Wichitas held a ritual in which they throw an axe into the ground, splitting the storm so it will go around the tribe. Some used a "cedaring ceremony" in which the smoke from a smoldering cedar tree is used to bless and protect the people.

But Indian lands were not totally immune. In May 2010 several homes on land managed by the Absentee Shawnee Tribal Housing Authority were damaged by a tornado. And in April of 2013 a tornado touched down near the Quapaw Tribe, destroying about 30 homes and buildings.

The worst storm in Matea's memory was the 1999 Bridge Creek-Moore Tornado. He'd been about six-years-old at the time. An extremely powerful EF5, it devastated portions of Oklahoma City and nearby towns, killing 36 people during an 85-minute rampage. The May 3rd Tornado (as it became known locally) produced the highest wind speeds ever globally recorded, a frightening 301 ± 20 MPH!

Nonetheless, tribal elders will tell you that tornados are easy to spot if you listen to the world around you. "Nature will tell you that a tornado is coming," Matea's father taught him. "The leaves of the trees whisper warnings, flipping themselves over in supplication to the angry skies. The birds warn by quieting their songs. Livestock file to far ends of fenced-in fields to escape a storm they know is coming."

But Matea did not have that listening skill. This tornado that hit Caruthers Corners seemed to come without any warning. Matea Davis was as surprised by it as anyone.

~ ~ ~

WZUR reporter Lucius Plancus interviewed meteorologist Stuart Frumkin. The weatherman explained that tornados are rare this late in the year because there usually isn't enough heat from the sun to sustain the thunderstorms. However, recent temperatures had been unseasonably warm, reaching into the 60s and 70s, warm enough to help produce severe weather when coupled with winds.

"You don't need temperatures in the 80s and 90s to produce severe weather," Frumkin said, "because this time of year the strong winds compensate for the lack of heating. That sets the stage for wind shear, which can produce tornados."

Each tornado is an isolated column of wind, he pointed out. Even so, tornados can be part of larger systems known as Super Cells. Such formations can produce swarms of tornados over a large geographic area.

According to National Weather Service records, Indiana has suffered major damage and loss of life from three of these Super Cells in modern times.

CHAPTER TWENTY-TWO

Side Trips

Bootsie drove over to the animal shelter to make sure the volunteers were taking care of the dogs and cats. She'd already circled by her home out near Old MacDonald's Dairy to make sure her own three canines were okay. Inka, Dinka, and Doo were still trembling, so she put on their Thunder Shirts to help calm them down and fed them bowls of Kibble.

Bootsie had driven her husband to work this morning, getting caught at the Town Hall when the storm hit. She was so relieved her pets were okay.

At the shelter, Bootsie found two of the volunteers and that Elwood boy who helped with the feedings. Everything looked under control. So she headed over to the Bentley farm to check on Cookie and Ben. That new deputy had assured her they were all right, but she wanted to see for herself.

The road was all but impassable, what with scattered tree limbs and downed power lines and automobiles upside down on the two-lane asphalt. She took the Field Hand Road detour, missing Cookie who had been heading into town by Highway 101.

Bootsie found Ben over at the Haney Bros. Zoo helping Bombay Martinez with the exotic animals. Feeding a tiger was a little more challenging than feeding, say, a Basset Hound.

"The animals are fine," Ben reassured her. "Happy's a little nervous, but Bombay is good at calming her down. That pachyderm follows him around like a big puppy dog."

"I'll say," observed Bootsie as the handler and his oversized pet ambled their way. "Biggest dog I've got at the shelter is a Saint Bernard. If nobody takes him, I may adopt him myself."

"That's good of you," Ben said. Thinking, Jim Purdue might have something to say about that. Their small house was already overrun with the three dogs they'd taken in.

"Where's Cookie?"

"She drove into town to check on everybody. I'm surprised you didn't pass her on the road."

"I took Field Hand Road. She probably took 101."

Ben nodded. "Yeah, that's the way she usually goes."

"Hullo, Mizz Bootsie," greeted Bombay as he walked up to her car, elephant following him. For years the Mexican had passed himself off as a Swami mind reader. Put on a turban and the rubes couldn't tell a Central American Indian from an East Indian. But it was all in the spirit of entertainment. These days he preferred working with the animals. Besides, his memory wasn't all that good anymore.

"How are the people at the Circus Retirement Home?" she asked Bombay. He lived there in a back cottage.

"A-Okay," he held up a thumb. "That big vacuum cleaner in the sky missed us, but it struck just up the street. I saw it lift up Ivor Yokovich's house just like

Dorothy's farmhouse in *The Wizard of Oz*. Old Ivor was in it. Don't know we'll ever see him again."

Ben kept his mouth shut. Ivor Yokovich was a wicked old cuss. No big loss, he thought to himself. But he didn't wish that kind of death on anybody. Even a dyspeptic old Azerbaijanian who spoke an unintelligible Russian dialect and probably admired Putin.

Bootsie nodded, "Good to know everybody at the retirement home's safe."

"Well, we're not sure about Big Bill Haney," Ben said. "The old fellow's missing. He went out for an early morning walk and nobody's seen him since."

~ ~ ~

Donald Smyth met with two of his employees at the Dollar General. Brenda Sprunger had been a cashier there for years, even back when it had been a Family Dollar store before Dollar General took it over. Matea Davis was a newbie, a stock boy who claimed to be a full-bloodied Potawatomi. Those were the Native Americans who occupied this section of Indiana back when it properly had been known as Indian Territory.

"Okay, Matea, there's some plywood in the back. Nail it over that broken window up front before someone decides to turn looter. Brenda, you put out a sign that says OPEN FOR BUSINESS. You can find plastic signs at the end of Aisle Three. We're probably going to have a run on tools and clean-up supplies today."

"Food Lion will be doing heavy business," said Brenda Sprunger. "Luckily, it wasn't in the tornado's path."

"Home Depot too," added Matea.

"A miracle we're still standing," Smyth said of the Dollar General. "The building next door is completely gone. And on the other side of us, the Dairy Queen has blown away – hey diddle diddle, like the cow who jumped over the moon."

"*Kche Mnedo* is watching over us," muttered Matea.

"Hey, don't give me none of that Injun mumbo jumbo. It was God's will."

"That's what I said."

"The First Mennonite Church was spared," observed Brenda Sprunger, a devout member. "But the parsonage is just a pile of rubble. Rev. Durrenberger and his wife are missing."

"There, there, Brenda. I'm sure the Reverend and his missus are all right. The Lord watches over his own."

"Amen," she said.

"*Ape iw nomikuk*," muttered Matea. "Amen" in the Potawatomi language.

~ ~ ~

Help began to arrive. At 2 p.m. Indiana National Guard trucks started rolling into Caruthers Corners. FEMA trailers began to appear by 3:15. The American Red Cross had already set up three stations around town.

Mayor Mark Tidemore was scheduled to appear on CNN at 5 o'clock. Lester Holt wanted him to do a phone-in for NBC's 6:30 news. He also had promised to give Lucius Plancus a live interview at 7 (curfew or not).

Fire Chief Freddie Madison's paramedics were still ferrying injured people to the Burpyville hospital. Yost & Yost had more bodies than they could handle, so they were shipping the overload down to a bigger funeral home in Pitsville.

The murder of Martin Lorenzo Griffith was all but forgotten.

CHAPTER TWENTY-THREE

Gimme Shelter

Leaving her car at the Town Hall, Cookie walked over to the Red Cross shelter on Fourth Avenue and signed up to be a volunteer at the food tent. Stacks of MRE's in flat foam containers already filled the back of the tent. Cartons of water bottles took up an equal amount of space. The big canvas tent had been set up in US Post Office's big parking lot. Everybody seemed to be dutifully ignoring the two mail trucks "parked" on the PO's roof.

People were already milling around, waiting for the handouts to begin. It was nearly 4 o'clock and people were eager for a hot lunch. There was a dazed look in many eyes, like *Night of the Living Dead* zombies shuffling about without direction. They just knew food was to be found somewhere nearby.

Dr. Smithy Oakman, assistant curator at the Perricock Museum of Science and History, joined Cookie at the food line. Smithy had volunteered to help serve. She and her husband lived in a far wing of the Museum, an impregnable stone monolith overlooking the town. The tornado had not reached it, petering out at the foot of the hill.

"This is some fine kettle of fish," said Smithy, referring to the aftermath of the tornado. "I was supposed to give a talk at the International Explorers Club in Indy today." The petite blonde was wearing her usual outfit, khaki slacks and a green safari shirt with many pockets and epaulets. She looked as if she'd just stepped off the Serengeti Plains.

"Threw off my schedule too," Cookie said. "My friends and I were just starting to look into the murder of that high school teacher."

"You girls have a strange hobby." The Quilters Club's sleuthing activities were well reported in the *Burpyville Gazette*. They were developing a kind of local celebrity aura, a pack of overaged Nancy Drews.

Cookie shrugged. "Quilting, playing detective, and history – those are my wheel spokes."

"And yet you find time to volunteer with the Red Cross."

"It's a good organization. The Red Cross has been helping people since 1863. Clara Barton started the American branch in 1881. Now, with 115 million volunteers in 186 countries, the Red Cross has won more Nobel Peace Prizes than anyone else in the world."

"You sure know your facts."

"A memory trick," Cookie said. Although in truth it was more of a "trick memory." Then she changed the subject: "Why are you volunteering?"

"Like the brochures say, the Red Cross provides a safe place to stay, food to eat, and a shoulder to lean on. I like being a part of that."

"The crowd looks hungry. What's on the menu today?"

"Here we have hamburgers, beans, juice," listed Smithy.

"What about that line over there?"

"That's where you can get emergency items that have been donated: Canned foods with pull-tops, peanut butter, granola bars, as well as toiletries, paper goods, diapers, and cleaning supplies."

Cookie's attention shifted to the crowd. "Wait, who is –?"

"Who is what?"

"Nothing. For a moment, I thought I saw an old high school teacher of mine."

~ ~ ~

"I don't get it," Aggie was saying to her friend Pricilla Moretz. "Everybody seems to have forgotten about that crazy actor killing Marty."

The two girls had met at one of the Red Cross tents. Volunteers were starting to serve hot meals to people displaced by the storm. She could see her Aunt Cookie standing over there with Smithy Oakman. They had their hands full, doling out Styrofoam boxes to the rowdy line of people.

Nearby was a large canvas tent filled with low cots, providing shelter for the homeless. Pricilla and her family would be bunking there tonight. As soon as her father could rent a car they would be going to stay with her aunt in Pitsville.

The Red Cross responds to approximately 64,000 disasters in the United States every year, ranging from home fires that affect a single family, to hurricanes that affect tens of thousands, to earthquakes that impact millions. Although not a governmental agency, the Red Cross provides shelter, food, and health services to help families and entire communities get back on their feet.

"Mr. Griffith's death was sad," replied Aggie's friend. Prissy Moretz and Teddy DiMacchio often double-dated with Aggie and Bobby. "But let's face it – life must go on."

Aggie knew it was hard to focus on the death of one individual when dozens of their friends and neighbors had died in this terrible tornado. But she still felt some kind of responsibility to remember Martin Lorenzo Griffith. He was fairly new to Caruthers Corners, but his life had already made an impact ... at least on her.

Aggie said, "Don't you wonder why that guy Robert De Niro did it?"

"Does it matter? Mr. Griffith's dead. Nothing will change that."

Aggie tried again. "I mean, there are so many unanswered questions about Marty's death. Aren't you curious why that guy shot him? Was he planning to shoot all of us? What was Marty's death all about?"

"Fortunately, those two football goons subdued that maniac. So we don't have to worry about what he had in mind. Now we've got bigger things to worry about. My home is gone. So is yours. Two of our neighbors down the street were killed by the storm. And my dad's taking us to Aunt Carol's. I don't know when I'll see my boyfriend again. Me and Teddy D were getting pretty serious. I was thinking of giving it up to him. Aren't you about ready to do it with Bobby?"

"No," said Aggie quickly. "I'm too young for that. Bobby and I are just friends."

"I was thinking I might drop out of school and marry Teddy D when he graduates next year." Teddy

DiMacchio was two grades ahead of them, the one with a driver's license.

"Are you insane? What about college."

"Aw, who needs that?"

"I do. My cousin N'yen and I have college trust funds. It would be a shame to waste the opportunity."

"Good for you. But I want to marry Teddy and move somewhere it's safe. Away from Tornado Alley."

Aggie shook her head. "Nowhere's safe, Prissy. Florida gets hurricanes. California gets earthquakes and mudslides. Colorado gets wildfires. New York gets terrorists."

"Yeah, and Alaska gets frostbite. Well, here I am living in a tent. That's a bad enough experience for me."

By nightfall the rows of Red Cross cots would take in more than 1,000 locals who had lost their homes.

~ ~ ~

Bobby Elwood caught up with Aggie as she walked toward the Town Hall. Curfew was coming up, so Aggie had planned on getting a ride home with her dad ... although "home" didn't quite apply. The blue Victorian facing the park was gone, only planks and plaster and tufts of pink fiberglass insulation to mark the spot where it stood for over 100 years. She had no idea where her family would be spending the night. She felt like a Syrian refugee.

"Hi Aggie. You okay?"

"Not really. You've seen what's left of my home. Splinters. Everything I had is gone – even my history term paper."

"That's not due for months."

"Yeah, but I wanted to get a head start. My Aunt Cookie had been helping me research it."

"What was your topic?"

"Indiana during the Civil War."

"Wow! That's a pretty big bite of history."

"Actually, it's very interesting. Indiana played an important role in supporting the Union. The state supplied more than 210,000 Union soldiers, sailors, and marines. These troops served in 308 military engagements during the war; the majority of them battles taking place between the Mississippi River and the Appalachian Mountains. War-related deaths exceeded 25,000."

"You sure know your beans. Sounds like an A+ paper to me."

"It would have been. But every word of it blew away with that tornado. So I've got to start over from scratch. Once I get a new computer."

"Don't feel so bad," sighed Bobby. "I haven't even picked a topic yet."

~ ~ ~

Thelma Ann König had been working at the Dairy Queen for the past year, up to the time the tornado hit. Now there wasn't a slanted-roof structure with soft-serve ice cream machines or freezers filled with Dilly Bars – just a flat cement slab left behind as reminder of warm summer afternoons.

Fortunately, Thelma Ann had been home at that early hour, still curled up in bed, covers tangled around her like a shroud. She was a fitful sleeper. Nevertheless, she came awake when she heard the sound, a roar like an approaching freight train. What the heck? She was frightened by the proximity of the noise.

She'd been on the job at the DQ less than a year. Serving banana splits, Blizzards, cherry Cokes, and mustard-laden hot dogs. A graduate of Caruthers High ("Go Melons!") this was her first job. She'd been doing well. A flirty blonde, the customers liked her.

Her house on Jinks Lane (she lived with her widowed mom) had been spared but no such luck for the DQ. Now she was out of work. Bummer.

Maybe her boyfriend could give her a job. He was a local businessman with several employees. What was one more? His wife would never know.

~ ~ ~

Big Bill Haney turned up. The former circus ringmaster was getting a little senile, his cognitive powers taking a sharp downward turn following the recent death of his wife. Deputy Truehart found him wandering along the highway up near Gruesome Gorge State Park. He said he was taking Sneezy the baboon for a walk. Fortunately, Sneezy was still at the zoo.

The recovery of Big Bill didn't change the estimated death toll. A hobo was found crushed under an overturned semi out on the 101 Bypass. The count remained at 37.

That included the bodies of Rev. Durrenberger and his wife, found under the piles of stones that was the parsonage. Also, Martha Eldridge died in her collapsed basement where she'd taken shelter from the storm. One of the dead bodies found under the rubble was identified as Tom Accola by dental records. Another turned out to be Little Timmy Wertzel. The Klondyke family was never found – not a single one of them.

This may have been the most painful day in the town's 189-year history.

CHAPTER TWENTY-FOUR

View From the Top

Limited phone service had been restored by late afternoon. From the Town Hall, Maddy phoned her son Bill in Chicago to let him know the family was okay. Bill's adopted son N'yen insisted on talking with Aggie. The two were best-est of friends, although they hadn't seen each other lately, him back in Chi-Town, her here.

N'yen was two years younger than his fifteen-year-old cousin. Although the little genius had skipped two grades as part of an Advanced Placement program, he was still a kid when it came to social skills. He resented her boyfriend, Bobby Elwood. N'yen worried that he and Aggie had been growing apart ever since she began dating.

But when he got her on the phone, he didn't care that she chattered on about how Bobby and his family were safe. Or about that teacher she'd had a crush on, the dead one. Or how Caruthers Corners ought to be called "the Windy City" instead of Chicago. He was just happy to hear her voice.

Needless to say, it was distressing news that Grammy and Grampy's house had been blown away. He'd left his favorite bike there, a GT Grade Carbon Ultegra 11-Speed. And Aggie's home – the Taylor Mansion, it'd been called – was gone too. He had liked sitting with his cousin on the front porch of that big blue Victorian house listening to live music from the bandstand across the street in the Town Square. And watching the Ferris wheel turn in the distance. He wasn't a big fan of heights, but he hated to think of the 70-foot-tall wheel being gone forever. Lighted up at night, turning in a slow hypnotic circle, it had reminded him of a magical Fairy Ring.

"At least all the Quilters Club members are safe," Aggie concluded breathlessly.

"Gee, I guess you guys don't have any crimes to solve, what with that big twister ripping through town," he added, almost as an afterthought.

"*Au contraire, mon frère,*" she said. Showing off her French 101, one of this year's classes. "We have not *un* but *deux* mysteries. The first, figuring out why a man who calls himself Robert De Niro killed my film professor. Shot him in front of the whole class. And the second, catching the person who stole a valuable 1925 Marie Webster quilt from Aunt Lizzie's museum this morning."

"Wow! You have lots of action down there in Indiana. A murder, a robbery, and a tornado. Wish I could be there with you!"

"Now that phone service had been restored, you can pitch in. You know, be our foreign correspondent."

"Foreign correspondent? Are you saying that 'cause I'm Asian?"

"No, silly. Because you're far away."

~ ~ ~

From her third-floor bedroom window, Hilda Hoople could see the entire town, spread out before her like the toy village of an electric train set. She could clearly see the zigzag of the tornado's path, as if someone had pushed a giant lawnmower through the town, cutting its way through houses and office buildings and copses of oak trees and playgrounds. She'd later be amazed to learn that only 37 people had died. The devastation looked horrendous.

Hilda had mortality on her mind. She'd visited Doc Medford earlier in the week to see how a series of tests had turned out. The news wasn't good – Parkinson's Disease. Hilda was the last of the world-famous Hoople Quadruplets. The three girls and one boy had been on the covers of national magazines, made newspaper headlines around the world, even once been invited to the White House to meet President Dwight D. Eisenhower.

Their parents had been quite wealthy. But the Hoople Quadruples – as people called them – added to the family coffers with public appearances, ribbon-cuttings, and endorsements for toys, fruit juices, and a preteen clothing line. The Hoople Quadruplets Trust Fund made Hilda the wealthiest person in Caruthers Corners.

She would have been the end of the Hoople line, for neither she nor any of her siblings ever married. But not long ago it was discovered that her brother Herbie had sired two daughters out of wedlock by Sue Ann Polk. Twins, it turned out. Although they had been given away for adoption, Emily Polk had spilled the beans after her sister Sue Ann's passing. Now the girls – women actually – were Hoople heirs.

That made Hilda feel better.

But there was more than enough money for Madelyn and Margaret. Or Maddy and Maisie as they were known hereabouts.

Maybe there was another good purpose for some of that money, she told herself, as she gazed down on the demolished town.

~ ~ ~

Just before the 7 o'clock curfew, Hilda Hoople reached Maddy at the Town Hall. The old woman was phoning to invite both the Madison and Tidemore families to stay at the Hoople Mansion. There was plenty of room, she pointed out. The huge 52-room manor that once had been home to the famous quadruples was now occupied only by Aunt Hilda and her new caretaker.

Maddy breathed a sigh of relief. Sleeping in a Red Cross shelter did not appeal to her delicate sensibilities. She preferred a Tempur-pedic Supreme Breeze mattress to a temporary hard-surface military cot.

CHAPTER TWENTY-FIVE

Sign Off

Lucius Plancus signed off at 9 p.m. with his final on-site broadcast for the day:

> *"Several blocks of houses have been erased from the landscape in this rural community of 3,000 watermelon farmers and small business owners. Indiana State Trooper Dustin Poulty, 37, said the tornado cut a path from one end of town to the other, knocking down power lines, uprooting trees, and rupturing gas lines. By nightfall, Trooper Poulty said there were reports of looting in the downtown area. The Dollar General experienced heavy losses. Mike's Sporting Goods reported losses that included guns, two camping tents, and a barbeque grill. Home Depot had a high amount of pilferage, also. The National Guard is having difficulty maintaining the curfew. State Troopers are supplementing their efforts."*

Being a member of the news media, the Jolly Red Giant had been issued a pass that exempted him from the curfew. After his broadcast, he called the station to get any feedback from the manager.

The good news: WZUR was receiving a high volume of calls from its listeners. They liked the radio station's On the Ground coverage of the tornado damage. People were hungry for firsthand news from the Disaster Area.

Several advertisers had phoned the station, upping their ad schedule, booking time adjacent to the live broadcasts from Caruthers Corners. New advertisers were lining up.

Lucius Plancus was a star.

~ ~ ~

CNN was calling it "the 2018 Northeast Indiana Tornado." Local folks merely referred to it as "the Twister." Some added expletives to that expression.

Anderson Cooper flew out to report on site. His recognizable white hair drew whistles from admiring fans. Despite being in a red Trump state, Caruthers Corners was fairly neutral in its political bent. Nobody called CNN "fake news" … or badmouthed former Indiana governor Mike Pence. A peaceful co-existence, of sorts.

The Weather Channel was there too, doing a piece on Storm Chasers, a profession romanticized by that 1996 movie *Twister*. The once-cutting-edge special effects in that film lost a little luster to locals who now had experienced the real thing.

An Indy TV station dug up a distant relative of L. Frank Baum, author of *The Wonderful Wizard of Oz*, for an exclusive interview. As if this blood relative knew anything about tornados or Emerald Cities.

"Mr. Baum," the coiffed anchorman asked a bewhiskered gentleman known by the mouthful of Oscar Zoroaster Phadrig Isaac Norman Henkle Emmannuel Ambroise Diggs Baum, "can I assume you got your lengthy nomenclature from *The Wonderful Wizard of Oz?*"

"Isn't it obvious?" The man seemed quite bored with the questions.

"Have you ever been in a tornado?"

"No."

"Do you wish one could carry you to the Land of Oz?"

"No."

"Are there any observations you'd like to make of your distant cousin's description of a tornado in his classic book?"

"No."

"Well, thank you for being with us today. It's been a pleasure talking with you."

PART III

"Well," said the Cowardly Lion, drawing a long breath of relief, "I see we are going to live a little while longer, and I am glad of it, for it must be a very uncomfortable thing not to be alive. Those creatures frightened me so badly that my heart is beating yet."

"Ah," said the Tin Woodman sadly, "I wish I had a heart to beat."

- L. Frank Baum,
The Wonderful Wizard of Oz

CHAPTER TWENTY-SIX

Philanthropical Activities

First thing next morning a long black limousine crawled into town, weaving its way around downed trees and timbers from damaged houses, slowly making its way up Hoople Hill toward the gabled stone mansion at the top. The suave, well-dressed man in the backseat was Barnabas Soltairé, Esq., administrator for the $800-million Hoople Quadruplets Trust Fund. Hilda Hoople had phoned him last night, saying she wanted to make a few adjustments in the fund's philanthropic disbursements.

With his impeccable credentials, Barnabas Soltairé had no trouble getting through the National Guard roadblock. One phone call to the Hoople Mansion and his driver was waved to proceed.

Hilda got down to business right away. She wanted to set aside enough money for her long-term care. Parkinson's could drag out. She could become totally disabled. So there needed to be funds for her and the caretaker.

Also, she wanted to take care of her only known relatives, Madelyn Agnes Hoople Taylor Madison and Maddy's twin sister Margaret Alice Walters. Something more than the trust funds they had already been given.

But mainly, after viewing this tornado disaster, she intended to share the rest of the Hoople fortune with the town of Caruthers Corners. A $600-million rebuilding fund, that was what she had in mind.

Barnabas would take care of the necessary paperwork.

~ ~ ~

Bobby Ray Purdue – one of the so-called Lost Boys, a trio of local youth who had disappeared into the Never Ending Swamp back in 1982, only to return with a traveling circus years later – was the second most wealthy person in town. While squandering some of it on such fanciful collectibles as a rare WWII biplane, an assortment of pinball machines, a stuffed grizzly bear, and a fleet of classic Indian motorcycles, he was also the philanthropist behind the petting zoo and the circus performers' retirement home, as well as several other good works hereabouts.

By noon on the day after the tornado he'd bought the entire inventory of the local Food Lion and posted a sign that said, FREE FOOD.

~ ~ ~

N.L. Purdue – owner of the demolished E-Z Seat chair factory – announced that all his employee would continue to draw their salaries while he rebuilt.

"You folks made me rich," he said. "Now I'm going to give some of that money back to you." Bobby Ray's older brother was known to be a greedy avaricious taskmaster, but for once his heart was in the right place.

The Weavers Union and the Woodworkers Union both voted to take a 20% pay cut till the company was "back on its feet" – a bit of a mixed metaphor, especially for a chair company.

~ ~ ~

Ben Bentley had provided a tract of land on the other side of town for FEMA to set up house trailers for the homeless. Somebody named it "Bentleyville" in honor of the donor. Ben was the second largest landholder in the county, next to Boyd Aikens.

Boyd did his part too. He used his fleet of watermelon trucks to haul in bottled water. It was being handed out by the case in the parking lot behind Town Hall.

~ ~ ~

Darnell Watson put together a crew to clear the streets and patch the broken asphalt. Darnell had the contract for snowplowing with the town, but during the summer he patched potholes and repaired cracked sidewalks. Lots of Boyd Aitkens's watermelon pickers were volunteering to help Darnell's street cleanup efforts.

Piles of debris were lining the street for removal. Planks and boards and refrigerators and sofas and mattresses and water heaters and rags and discarded clothing – all waiting to be hauled way. Mayor Tidemore had already contracted with Wally's Waste Removal down in Pitsville to help clear away the mounds of wreckage.

~ ~ ~

Before the tornado struck, Lucius Plancus had been assigned to cover the murder of that teacher at Caruthers Corners. That happenstance had put him at Ground Zero for the disaster coverage ahead of all the other news teams – radio, TV, print. He was Johnny on the Spot. Lucky Lucius, he co-workers started calling him.

The tornado had been a much bigger news story than the murder, with nearly two score of people killed by the twister. His coverage of the event was sure to make his career.

Now, it was time to turn his attention back to the original assignment. But when Lucius Plancus finally got over to the police department to interview the alleged murderer of Martin Lorenzo Griffith, the holding cell was empty.

"Did the bugger escape?" he exclaimed. Thinking this might be a journalistic bonanza, a murderer on the run on top of this tornado story.

"Nobody escapes when I'm on duty," said Deputy Pete Hitzer. He'd never liked this pushy carrot-topped reporter. Maybe it was the size difference. Petie was a skinny ragdoll of a man; Lucius a 300-pound giant.

"So, where is he?"

"Out on bail."

"There's no bail for murder."

Petie shrugged. "Tell that to Judge Bristol. He signed off on Black getting released. Some Burpyville shyster showed up with a Writ of Habeas Corpus."

"Wait a minute. That's is a claim of unlawful detention. As I understand it, you had solid grounds for an arrest. More than a dozen eyewitnesses to the murder." As a graduate of Indiana State, Plancus knew that *habeas corpus* was Medieval Latin for "that you have the body" – a demand that you produce a prisoner to the court to determine if the charges were lawful, to demonstrate you had a body of evidence to indicate possible guilt.

"Beats me. I just arrest 'em. The judge and jury does the rest."

"But there may not be a jury trial if the judge released him on *habeas corpus*. Who's this genius lawyer that got him out?"

"A shyster from Burpyville by the name of J. Harold Wentworth. From what I hear, he's just an inch from being disbarred. It's a safe bet he's gonna do some jail time for embezzlement of escrow accounts. Unless he can pull a rabbit out of a hat for himself, like he did for that guy Robert De Niro."

"Robert De Niro, my foot. We both know this guy's not the actor from those *Meet the Parents* movies."

"No," confirmed Petie. "We just got his prints back. Turns out his real name is Robert Dietrich Black. That didn't surprise me. I mean, what's the likelihood of two actors being named Robert De Niro?"

CHAPTER TWENTY-SEVEN

Searching

Matea Davis volunteered to help with the search and rescue. There was still lots of rubble to sift through. The manager at Dollar General gave him the time off to join the cleanup operation. The discount store remained open, but there was no inventory left to put on the shelves. Looters had practically cleaned them out. So Donald Smyth figured he could spare the new stock boy for a few days. Time off without pay, that would make up for what Thelma Ann was costing the store.

First thing, Matea checked on the families of his Badger Patrol campers. As the new troop leader, he took his role very seriously. Of the dozen members – actually ten since N'yen Madison went back to Chicago and Georgie Yager moved away with his mother – three of them had lost their homes. Bobby Bjorn and his folks had taken sanctuary in a FEMA trailer out near the petting zoo. Kinky Osbourn's family was staying at a Red Cross shelter. And then there was Stewie Klondyke, a 12-year-old corporal in the Badger Patrol.

The entire Klondyke family – Stewie, his dad and mom – was unaccounted for. The plot of land where their house once stood was now a vacant lot. The foundation blocks traced the shape of the three-bedroom ranch-style house. There had been no storm cellar.

Matea had known Sam Klondyke pretty well. Sam was the day manager for ZapData, a tech company located in the Industrial Park. The two men used to chat when Matea had worked as the night watchman out there.

Where were the Klondykes and their beautiful brick home? Hard to say. Scientists will tell you there's no way to predict where a tornado might deposit objects swept up by its rotating funnel. A swirling mass of wind and rain, a twister could sling detritus in any direction. Toss cars like Matchbook toys. Shred houses to splinters. Knock structures over. Or deposit the ruins miles away.

Bricks left a trail up Melon Ball Boulevard. Madea tried to follow the red clay blocks, like Hansel and Gretel tracking bread crumbs through the forest. But eventually the bricks became farther and farther apart, then disappeared altogether.

The Klondykes – all three of them – were presumed dead.

~ ~ ~

The National Guard soldiers went about the search methodically. They marked off a grid on a 1:50,000-scale military topographic map. Each section was searched, then marked off as clear. A way of being sure that no spot got overlooked.

No new dead bodies were found. But there were a few rescues.

The Adelphi family had been found trapped in their storm cellar. Two Simpson sisters were found hiding in their closet. An 80-year-old lady named Rita Rutaberger was discovered lying on her kitchen floor with a broken hip. One of Andrew Linderman's nine children was sighted walking up Watermelon Seed Alley without a diaper; the family hadn't even noticed that 2-year-old Emmanuel was missing.

Finally, having covered every inch of the town, the Guardsmen regrouped and resumed patrol. There were no new reports of looting. Last night's culprits had been arrested, most of them members of the notorious Crackleton clan. Granny Crackleton's brother Ed's delinquent boys.

The National Guard set up their own stockade, so Police Chief Jim Purdue's two holding cells remained empty (the last occupant having been Robert Di Nero).

~ ~ ~

Odell Lumley hadn't continued his investigation into the finances of Martin Lorenzo Griffith. After all, he no longer had a client. But he couldn't help being concerned when he read in the newspaper about Griffith's death, allegedly at the hands of his former client.

He checked on Griffith's estate, out of curiosity. There had been a will, leaving everything to a sister. A total of $112 (there had been cash in his wallet), $1,000 in stocks, and a few personal items. Nothing approaching $200,000.

Perhaps he was getting sloppy, Lumley told himself, He'd missed those stocks in his earlier snooping. The sister had been holding them. Could she have been holding the $200 grand also?

What the heck, he took a look at her finances. But there was nothing there. Her husband was a tie salesman at Macy's in New York City. The couple had very little savings and carried a large mortgage for a two-bedroom house in Queens. No big sums bouncing about in their bank account.

So where was the money?

Or maybe there was no money, that it was merely a mental fiction of Robert Di Nero. The man was obviously demented.

However, the PI did discover one interesting fact: His client had not been Robert Di Nero at all. The man's birth certificate identified him as Robert Dietrich Black, born in Manchester, New Hampshire, to a steam-plant pipefitter and his schoolteacher wife. Both deceased.

For a moment, Lumley wondered if shooting a schoolteacher was some kind of Oedipal Complex directed at his mother?

But then he remember the elusive $200,000 – supposedly stolen from a group of Toledo dentists -- and figured it went back to that age-old adage: Follow the money!

~ ~ ~

Later that afternoon Barnabas Soltairé made an announcement that the Hoople Quadruplets Trust Fund would be donating $600 million to the town's rebuilding. The project would be called the Caruthers Corners Restoration Coalition. The Coalition would rebuild every single home and commercial building destroyed by the 2018 Northeast Indiana Tornado.

What's more, each family that lost a home would receive a $10,000 grant to cover temporary housing and living expenses.

Barnabas Soltairé stood on the steps of the Town Hall as he revealed the plan. A crowd of 200 or 300 people had gathered, filling the street and spilling onto the edge of the park. Several TV cameras were visible. Lucius Plancus was there with a digital recorder.

Soltairé had timed it so the feed could make the 6:30 NBC News. CNN and Fox would run it at will. WZUR was broadcasting live.

There was lots of applause.

You would've thought Hilda Hoople was close to being canonized. People compared her to Mother Teresa. Someone suggested naming a holiday after her. She was hero of the day, no question about that.

The announcement ran into overtime. Folks barely had time to get home, or to a Red Cross shelter, before the curfew set in.

CHAPTER TWENTY-EIGHT

Open For Business

Despite the rubble still left behind by the tornado, Cozy Café was open for business by the next morning. Everything on the menu was half-off for local residents.

Maisie Walters had survived the storm, her tiny little home being three blocks off the twister's path through town. Despite her modest lifestyle, Maisie could afford to be generous with her customers. Like her twin sister Maddy, she had a sizable trust fund from the Hoople estate. So she anonymously paid Yost & Yost for the funeral expenses of all 37 people who had died in the storm.

Maisie especially felt bad about the death of Big Nose Evans. She'd dated him in high school. And the death of Elsie Warton hit her hard too. Elsie had been a neighbor, her house just behind the diner. The path of the tornado had been *that* close, within 20 feet. In addition to paying Elsie's funeral expenses, she'd adopted her cat. Alexander the Great spent more time atop the diner's trash cans than he did at home – a fact that likely saved the big tabby from the deadly twister.

On Day Three, National Guard trucks still rumbled along Main Street. According to new reports, 48 people remained in the Burpyville hospital recovering from storm-related injuries. The oddest one being Shorty Yosterman who'd had a plastic drinking straw pierce his arm like an arrow, due to the force of the cyclone's wind. Maisie vowed to switch to paper straws henceforth. Paper straws were both biodegradable and not as stiff as a crossbow bolt.

~ ~ ~

At precisely 8 a.m. the four adult members of the Quilters Club took their usual places in the corner booth at Cozy Café. Maisie delivered steaming cups of Maxwell House before the women had wiggled into the tight seating.

"I'm glad to see that you're all right," said Maddy to her sister. Fraternal twins, the two women looked nothing alike. Maddy with silver hair and rounded features; Maisie with sharp pinched features like Flo in those Progressive TV commercials.

"Missed me by a mile," Maisie smiled. "Well, by a quarter of a mile, to be more precise."

"Thank goodness."

"Where's Aggie?" Maisie asked. She knew the girl was the fifth member of the quilting group-cum-quasi-detective-agency.

"Oh, she'll be along shortly," said Maddy. "School is closed the rest of the week. Principal Zwicky was one of the casualties, you know."

"I heard. He was a nice guy. Came in for coffee on the weekends."

"The School Board has promoted the assistant principal. Angela Pawley takes over the high school starting next week," reported Lizzie. First with the town gossip. "Angelia's pretty broken up. She and Fred Zwicky were having a thing, it seems."

Maisie nodded knowingly. "I can confirm that. She always joined Fred here for coffee on Sunday mornings. They held hands under the counter."

"Hi everybody," came Aggie's cheerful voice. Leave it to Maddy's granddaughter to have an upbeat attitude in the middle of a Disaster Zone.

"Hi, Aggie," came a chorus of greetings from her friends.

"Sorry I'm late," she said, taking the chair that Maisie had pulled up for her at the end of the booth. The seating was still a little crowded with Bootsie off her diet. And given the stress of recent events there was little likelihood she'd be going back on Weight Watchers anytime soon.

"A watermelon juice?" asked Maisie, knowing it was Aggie's favorite.

"Thank you," she said, ever polite.

"Girls, we have to get that Marie Webster quilt back," Lizzie began with no further preamble. "I haven't reported the theft to the Indianapolis Museum of Art yet. If word gets out about its loss, our little quilting museum will be *kaput*."

"I agree," said Cookie. "Our reputation is at stake."

"We can't let some no-good burglar get away with stealing an irreplaceable quilt by a grand master like Marie Daugherty Webster," nodded Bootsie. Always the law-and-order member of the group.

"What about the murder of my teacher?" said Aggie.

"Hon, there's not much we can do about that. A lawyer has already sprung him," replied Bootsie.

"Right now, we have to concentrate of that missing quilt," insisted Lizzie.

"Let's think through this," said Maddy. "It seems to me that someone took advantage of the natural disaster to steal the quilt."

"So it was an opportunistic theft," nodded Bootsie.

"The storm may have given the thief cover, but he had to know it was there in the first place," observed Aggie. Trying to be helpful, despite her disappointment in the lack of interest in her teacher's death.

"Somebody local?" said Cookie.

"Very likely," nodded Maddy. "Lizzie doesn't even have the quilting museum's sign up yet. An out-of-towner wouldn't know what was there. On the outside it looks like any other house on the street."

"The sign's supposed to go up this Friday," sighed Lizzie. "But with this blasted tornado who knows when the sign company will deliver it."

"There's another piece of the puzzle," said Maddy. "You hadn't announced the exhibit yet. So who would know you had a rare Marie Webster quilt in the gallery?"

"Nobody. The ad for the 'Pink Dogwoods' show isn't scheduled to run in the *Burpyville Gazette* until Sunday."

"Somebody knew."

"That means the thief would have to be someone who works in the newspaper's ad department," Cookie stated the logical conclusions. "... or someone local that you've told."

"I've hardly told anyone," protested Lizzie. "Just you guys –"

"I think you can eliminate us as suspects," huffed Bootsie. Offended by the suggestion.

"– and our husbands."

"Ditto," said Bootsie.

"Other than you guys I haven't told anybody here in town. I wanted to surprise everybody, make a big splash for the quilting museum."

"Okay, somebody outside of town?" Cookie asked the obvious question.

"Let me think. I may have mentioned it to Margie Yost when I got my nails done last week." Margie owned the Helen of Troy Spa and Beauty Salon over in Burpyville. Prissy by nature, Lizzie had a standing weekly appointment.

"That means the whole world knows," sighed Bootsie. "Margie is Miss Information Central. Blabs to all her customer. Swapping your information for their information."

Lizzie held up her hands to inspect her nails. They were a shade called Robin's Breast Red – a bright hue that complimented her flaming-red hair. "Margie said she wanted to come to the opening on Monday night."

"Well, the opening's off for now," observed Maddy. "You don't have the quilt to show."

"True."

"You're saying the thief is a client of Helen of Troy?" Aggie tried to follow the logic.

"All her customers are women," said Maddy. "You said the door had been forced open with a crowbar. That's more like a man's work."

"Right," Lizzie nodded. "Jim Elwood and Sven Oberly saw a man breaking down the door."

"Maybe it was the husband of one of Margie's clients," suggested Bootsie.

"You mean partners in crime – like a Bonnie and Clyde?" said Aggie. Her imagination running away with her.

"Bonnie Parker and Clyde Barrow were bank robbers," Cookie pointed out. "Not burglars. And they weren't married."

"Well, you get the idea. Two burglars instead of one."

"That seems likely," Lizzie accepted the idea. "Most of Margie's clients are married."

"So we're talking about a local wife who gets her hair or nails done in Burpyville," Aggie tried to restate the theory. "She hears about the quilt from Blabbermouth Margie and tells her larcenous husband. Bing-bang-boom, they steal the quilt under the cover of the storm."

"Something like that," nodded Maddy. Proud of her granddaughter's detecting skills.

"Does Margie Yost have many clients from here?" Cookie continued the thought process.

"I'd guess she has a dozen or two," said Lizzie. Likelier to know, she went to the beauty salon on a more regular basis than her friends. Bootsie's pixie cut didn't take much upkeep. Maddy had let her hair go silver, so she only needed an occasional trim. And Cookie was content with her dishwater blonde mop, adding a few self-inflicted snips when it got too long.

"This is an interesting puzzle," sighed Aggie. Wishing her cousin N'yen were here to help them solve it. He could figure this out, she was convinced of that.

"Now what?" asked Bootsie. She always deferred decisions to the others.

"Let's make a beauty run," Maddy decided. "I think we need to get a facial."

CHAPTER TWENTY-NINE

Helen of Troy

They drove over to Burpyville after finishing their morning coffee. The road was open and uncluttered once you got outside of Caruthers Corners. The tornado's devastation had been confined to the town limits. An aerial view looked like someone had sliced the little burg in half with the jagged stroke of a dull knife.

It was an easy drive. Helen of Troy Spa and Beauty Salon was just off Highway 101 on the west side of Burpyville. A low one-story brick building, its location was announced by a large neon sign flashing **CHIC HAIRSTYLING**. With each flash, the word **CHIC** changed to **CUT-RATE**, then back again. The descriptor CHIC was a play on the word CHICK. And CUT-RATE was more about haircutting than a promise of economy.

Margie Yost was at the front counter going over today's bookings when they walked in. These days Margie didn't personally spend much time clipping hair and painting nails. A successful entrepreneur, she now had three full-time stylists working for her. The salon was throwing off a tidy profit – enough to keep up her payments on a brand-new Miami blue Porsche 911 Carrera 4S (sticker price $112,000). Success, by her definition.

Margie's own hairstyle was not recommended for clients. Her mane was as wide and fuzzy as an Afro, quite a feat of legerdemain for a white gal of Dutch origins. Yost is an Americanized spelling of the Dutch surname "Joost" or the Germanic version "Jost." Today, Margie's hair was dyed a bright green. And it wasn't even St. Patrick's Day.

"Hi, ladies," she greeted them. "Do you need a group appointment? Is there a big event coming up? I would've thought everything would be canceled after that awful tornado hitting your town. Are you all okay? Are your families all right? I've been worrying about you." Margie was a talker, a trait common to bartenders and beauticians.

"Maddy lost her house," Lizzie replied. She had the strongest relationship with Margie, being such a regular customer and all. She maintained a weekly appointment for hair and nails. "The rest of us escaped the worst."

"Maddy, I'm sorry to hear about your house. You've shown me pictures. It was an elegant old Victorian, as I recall. A historical home from the 1800s, right? Did you lose your belongings? Your car?"

"Everything," said Maddy. Not feeling like enumerating her losses. It was too sad to contemplate.

"Well, that's a downright shame. I don't know what I'd do if I lost everything. I wouldn't have anywhere to go. My mother doesn't have the room. And I don't get along with my sister's husband. He's a jerk. Do you know him? He runs the Dollar General over your way. Donnie Smyth. He puts on such airs, spelling Smyth with a *y*. I think he plays around on my sister."

"I know Donald," admitted Lizzie. "He's very friendly."

"Maybe a little too friendly, you ask me. He and Patricia have a kid. You'd think he'd stay home more. But he's always out prowling like a tomcat. He even made a pass at me once, his own sister-in-law. What nerve. But he is kinda cute with that broken nose."

Cookie said, "I know their son Buddy. He's in the Badger Patrol. My husband is head of the Sons of Anthony Wayne."

"I don't know why they call him Buddy. Nathan is a perfectly good name. It was my dad's name – Nathan Allen Yost. He died in that American Eagle crash back in 1994. Flight 4184 went down in a field near Roselawn. That's in western Indiana, near the Illinois border."

"Your father was on that flight?" said Cookie. Her super memory at play. "As I recall 68 people were on that plane."

"Oh, he wasn't on the plane. It fell on him. He was over there buying a cow. Then – *bam!* – out of nowhere this twin-engine turboprop ATR 72 falls on top of him. Killed the cow too."

"Sorry about that," muttered Cookie.

"Word is that your sister and her family are safe," added Bootsie, trying to get the conversation back on track.

"Yes, she called. They've got most of the phone service restored. Indiana Bell does a good job of keeping communications open. I remember back in –"

"We have a favor to ask," Maddy interrupted. Leave Margie Yost to her own devices, she'd talk your ear off.

"A favor –?"

"Yes, could you give us a list of your Caruthers Corners customers? It's for a case we're working on."

"Jeez, you gals are after another bad guy? That's exciting. You ought to hang out a shingle and become a real detective agency. Everybody says you're good at solving crimes."

"It's a knack," said Aggie. She'd almost been overlooked, standing there behind the grow-ups.

"Well, you Quilters Clubbers certainly have it. But I don't know if it would be ethical for me to share my customer list. People like their privacy. Remember, I couldn't give you a list a few years ago when you were looking for men who wore toupees."

"This isn't the same," argued Lizzie. "Men who wear a toupee may want to keep that a secret. But *all* women get their hair cut or styled from time to time. No need for privacy in that."

"You just want the ones who come to me from Caruthers Corners? Might be a dozen, not counting you gals. I can probably sort them out on my computer by zip code. I keep all my customers' addresses so I can send out flyers when I'm having a special on trims or dye jobs or whatever. Advertising pays off. I've doubled my revenues over the past two years – all thanks to advertising in the *Burpyville Gazette*."

"We'd really appreciate it if you'd do that – sort your list, I mean," said Maddy. Offering a wide coaxing smile.

"If you'll give us the list, I'll treat everybody to a facial," offered Lizzie. Kind of a bribe. "That is, if you've got enough girls on staff to handle all five of us."

"Gee, I've never had a facial before," said Aggie. Feeling very grown-up at that moment. A girl had to start thinking of her looks when she had a boyfriend, right?

"All three of my helpers are here. We can handle you. Let me get those facials started and then I'll check my computer for names."

But Margie was thinking, five facials at $120 a pop, a good morning's profit.

~ ~ ~

"When you book a facial," explained Margie Yost, "you're not just paying for an hour-long series of cleansers, masks and serums being applied to your face. The price tag reflects the expertise of the aesthetician performing your treatment."

"Aesthetician?" said Aggie.

"My professional facialists," explained Margie, indicating the three hairstylists lined up behind styling chairs in back. "They have a high level of training and technical expertise."

"Wow!" said the girl.

As it happened, Lizzie Ridenour was the only member of the Quilters Club who partook of regular facials. Bootsie Purdue had only had one or two. Cookie Bentley hadn't had one in years, eschewing that "I Feel Pretty" beauty queen thing. Maddy Madison only had facials on special occasions, like her birthday last year. And for Aggie, this would be her first time.

"There are many benefits of facials," continued Margie. "But for teens in particular facials help clean out blackheads and clogged pores caused by oil production. Most young people experience clogged pores, acne, and breakouts at some point during their teenage years."

"I've got pretty clear skin," protested Aggie. "Just a few freckles across my nose."

"Yes. And we want to keep it clear," nodded Margie, escorting the girl to a chair that looked like it came from the Starship *Enterprise*.

The assigned aesthetician began with a thorough cleansing of Aggie's skin using a foaming cleanser followed by exfoliation via microdermabrasion. Then came a series of masks tailored to the girl skin type. This included letting an exfoliator ("facial in a jar") work its magic for at least 10 or 15 minutes. The aesthetician finished off by layering serums and moisturizers to lock in the hydration.

Afterward, Aggie's skin glowed a healthy pink. And it felt baby-soft. She loved it!

Bootsie fell asleep during her facial. The aesthetician nudged her when she began to snore.

As for Cookie, she luxuriated in the treatment. She'd downplayed her looks for years, no longer considering herself beauty queen material – although you would never know that looking at her heart-shaped face and perfect bone structure.

Maddy did a facial complete with a peel. It left her looking like a boiled lobster, but that would fade in a day or so. She kept one eye on Margie Yost, making sure she was printing out the zip-code sorted customer list as promised.

Lizzie put the $750 (including tips) on her gold Amex card without blinking. It was nice to have a trust fund set up by your grandfather who founded a bank.

CHAPTER THIRTY

Margie's List

Of the 23 women on Margie Yost's customer list, seven were dead from the tornado. Two were off on a Caribbean cruise. The four members of the Quilters Club, of course, eliminated themselves. That left a list of ten people.

Two of the ten were septuagenarians, hardly candidates as kick-the-door-down burglars. Three more were single moms with no significant others to help them pull off a heist – still possibilities, but not likely. Another was Florence Kilroy, wife of the minister at Peaceful Meadows. She and her husband were not high on the suspect list.

Four to go.

Just back from Burpyville, they squeezed into the corner booth at Cozy Café. Aggie got the chair at the end. Without being asked, Maisie served up cups of Maxwell House for the grown-ups; a watermelon milkshake for Aggie.

Lizzie spread Margie's list on the Formica tabletop. "Okay, here we are. Only a few names to go."

"I know this woman," Bootsie pointed to the list. "Bitsy Smoot's salt of the earth. Teaches Sunday School. I can't believe she would steal a historic quilt. Besides, she's a widow. No man to help her break down the door."

"This one – Birdie Longstreet – she sings in the choir at St. Paul's United Methodist Church," Cookie said. "I know Birdie pretty well. I'd trust her with my purse any day of the week." Cookie was deeply involved with St. Paul's – a Professing member who took on the leadership role of a Certified Lay Servant. She knew the congregation extremely well so Cookie's endorsement was good enough for her friends.

"How about Natalie Scherzinger?" said Lizzie. "I see her name listed here. Natalie's husband is an ex-con. Those are the right credentials – one of Margie's customers who's married to a guy that's done jail time."

"True, Charlie Scherzinger served a year or two for bad checks," responded the police chief's wife. "However, Charlie's not a break-and-enter kind of guy. He's only been known to kite bad checks. White Collar Crimes, they call it."

"Duly noted," said Maddy. "That leaves one last name – Faith Ann Ritchie."

Lizzie looked up from her coffee, leaving red lipstick prints on the rim of the white ceramic cup. "Faith Ann – she's a Crackleton."

"Exactly."

The Crackletons were a notorious clan of crooks and physical freaks who had an enclave just north of town. Most people hereabouts tried to avoid them. The 98-year-old Sarah Celine Crackleton – better known as Granny – was matriarch of the crime family ... and Faith Ann's mother.

"Well –" hesitated Cookie. The subject was awkward for her. She and Ben were fostering Faith

Ann's youngest son, a kid named Augustus. Gus, for short.

"Bear with us, Cookie," urged Lizzie. "All the folks in that clan are crooks. Everybody knows that."

"Not Gus," protested Cookie. Feeling protective of her ten-year-old foster son's genetic heritage.

"That's because he's found a good home."

"Nurture trumps Nature," said Bootsie without any evidence one way or the other.

"Faith Ann is a single mother," argued Cookie. "She doesn't have a husband or boyfriend to help her with the burglary. It took some muscle behind that crowbar to pry open the museum's door."

"Aw, you know Faith Ann has plenty of cousins up there," said Bootsie. "Any one of them would be willing to break into the quilting museum if she asked."

"Cousins?" snorted Lizzie. "You mean brothers, uncles, baby daddies." The Crackletons were more inbred than California Show Dogs.

"I think we're being a little too hard on the Crackletons," pouted Cookie.

"Even so, you've got to admit Faith Ann is a reasonable suspect," said Maddy. "She stays on the list."

~ ~ ~

A number of Crackletons were doing prison time – thanks to the Quilters Club. So you could understand the suspicion the gals might have about the trashy family. Jeb Crackleton and his sons Dub, El, and Vis were incarcerated in various facilities around the state. Granny bore a grudge. It's a wonder Faith Ann agreed to let the Bentley's act as foster parents to her 10-year-old son Gus.

An august group of researchers had studied the Crackletons regarding results of their inbreeding. A number of abnormalities were recorded, from extra toes to prehensile tails, pinheads to prognathism.

Jed Crackleton was a giant of extraordinary height, his son Dub was a dwarf, his other sons El and Vis were separated conjoined twins. The entire family was a genetic mess.

Due to these freakish attributes, the Crackletons lived on the very edge of society for generations, allowing them to develop amoral lifestyles. Interfamilial relationships continued this in a never-ending cycle, ultimately producing a tribe of misfits, medical oddities, and thieves.

As a wise man once said, "A Crackleton would jus' as soon steal your watch as to ask you the time of day."

~ ~ ~

Out of curiosity, the private investigator checked Robert Black's bank account. He could break into Bank of America databases as easy as walking into the next room. The statements showed two large withdrawals.

- The first $10,000 was Lumley's fee. Nearly two weeks at $100 an hour.
- The next $25,000 went to a lawyer, J. Harold Wentworth in Burpyville.
- There was slightly less than $15,000 left in the account, the balance from the $50,000 he received for starring in that schlocky movie.

Odell Lumley thought about it. Black wouldn't last long on $15 grand. And he wouldn't be getting any acting jobs after that movie, *Three Funerals and Something-or-Another*. Ol' Bobby would likely keep looking for the missing $200,000. And he'd proved he was willing to kill to get it.

Dangerous times.

CHAPTER THIRTY-ONE

Living in a Castle

The Madisons and the Tidemores were quite comfortable in their respective wings of the Hoople Mansion. Hilda Hoople seemed to be pleased with the company. For years after her siblings passed away, she'd lived a reclusive existence, even pretending to be her own maid to avoid curiosity seekers. Back in the '60s and '70s the Hoople Quadruples had been quite famous, as you'll recall. Now, few people remembered them at all.

Aunt Hilda had hired a new maid. Well, actually, Marybelle Olsen was more of a caretaker. After all, Hilda Hoople had been diagnosed with Parkinson's Disease.

PD is a degenerative disorder of the central nervous system that affects the motor system. The symptoms increase over time. Early stages include shaking palsy, slowness of movement, and eventual dementia. Sometimes death it occurered.

But diminished capacity, any way you measured it.

Aware of the prognosis, Hilda Hoople had begun working with Barnabas Soltairé, administrator of the Hoople Quadruplets Trust Fund, to put her affairs in order. Money had been set aside for her long-term care.

Marybelle Olsen was part of Phase One. A companion of sorts.

Phase Two. A portion of the estate would be divided between Maddy and her twin sister Maisie. That had started with their trust funds.

Phase Three. The rest of the money would go toward rebuilding the town. At her request, Soltairé had already set up the Caruthers Corners Restoration Coalition. The name had a nice ring to it. And $600 million was enough to work with. Housing in Caruthers Corners was modest, except for the mansions on the hill. They had been untouched by the 2018 Northeast Indiana Tornado.

Aunt Hilda thought the Madisons' homeless status was a serendipitous opportunity to introduce them to living in the mansion. Eventually it would be theirs.

While the mansion would go to Maddy's side of the family, Maisie would receive a number of other real estate holdings, including the Wabash Acres housing development. Even-steven in value.

The Madisons and Tidemores seemed to be settling in. Aggie liked having her Grammy and Grampy down the hall. Much more convenient than living two blocks away. Her cousin N'yen would be so jealous when he learned she was living in the big stone mansion at the top of Hoople Hill.

Too bad this was only temporary. These lodgings were more comfortable than a posh hotel with a four-star Michelin rating.

~ ~ ~

That evening Aggie padded down to the kitchen in her jammies, looking for milk and watermelon cookies. She was surprised to find Marybelle Olsen there, preparing a pot of chamomile tea for Aunt Hilda.

"Hilda's having trouble getting to sleep," the caretaker said.

"Does tea help?"

Marybelle smiled pleasantly. "Chamomile is regarded as a mild tranquilizer or sleep inducer. For years, it has been used as a natural remedy to treat insomnia."

"Maybe I should have tea instead of cookies and milk."

"Are you having trouble sleeping?"

"Not really. But ever since the tornado I keep laying there in bed thinking of all the people who have died."

"Those people are fine. It's the ones left behind who need our prayers," the gray-haired woman said.

"That makes sense," the girl agreed, thinking over those sage words.

"You just have to look at the world with a smile on your face, then you'll see that it's a very happy place."

"Are you Mary Poppins?" Aggie asked.

~ ~ ~

Tilly liked living in the mansion. It made her feel like a princess in a castle. Ever since childhood, she had gazed up the hill at the big stone building with its many gables and smoking chimneys and high windows, and imagined it was a castle where a princess lived. Now she was that princess.

Even a grown woman could pretend, she told herself.

She liked being married to Mark, being mother of his four children, but even princesses could have a family. What did people think happened in those fairy tales after Cinderella met Prince Charming. You know, after the words *And she lived happily ever after....*"

Tilly had loved her home facing the Town Square. But the Taylor Mansion was no more. The big blue Victorian house had been blown somewhere over the rainbow. Thankfully, she and Mark and the children hadn't been in it at the time. The Town Hall where Mark worked was only half a block away. And its basement was one of the safest storm refuges in the entire town.

In the early 1800s Ferdinand Jinks had burned down the original Town Hall, a protest over Jacob Caruthers stealing the town's name. The structure had been rebuilt of brick, stronger and more solid than ever, with a basement dug into solid stone. This lower floor served as a handy storage depot for the town's records – property surveys, deeds, tax invoices, marriage records, birth and death certificates – like an underground Fort Knox. But it made for an even better storm cellar, capable of holding 250 people if crowded together.

A storage room down there held emergency supplies – big 4-gallon jugs of water, MRE packets, first aid kits, even radiation detectors -- a holdover from the '50s when schoolchildren were taught to "duck and cover" should Russian bombers appear overhead. Now the food and water, regularly replaced, served as tornado supplies. An assemblage of 250 people could last two weeks down there.

During the tornado, some 80 or 100 people had taken cover in the basement, the small number due to the short warning time. Tilly and the younger children were among them.

Tilly felt proud that her husband was mayor of Caruthers Corners. And a good one by all accounts. Her dad had been mayor before him, but he had been elected as a calming influence, "a breath of fresh air" following a long reign of terror and corruption by Henry Caruthers. Ol' Henry was a scion of a Founding Father, Jacob Abernathy Caruthers himself. Bad blood, some people said.

Tilly's dad had been descended from a Founding Father also, one Beauregard Hollingsworth Madison. Beau was the Fourth, both in numerical order and in name. The Madisons were well respected – a proud heritage.

Tilly's husband – Mark Raymond Tidemore – was descended from a poor family who settled here around the Turn of the Century. The surname of Tidmore comes from northern Germany. Records indicate that the name is a variation of Dietrich or Dieterich or Detmar. Chronicles first mention one Tidemannus (Tidercus) of Hamburg in 1262. The name acquired prominence due to its owners' contributions to medieval society.

Many Prussians migrated to North America in search of a new start during the 1800s. Philadelphia was their primary point of entry into the United States, with Nicholas Tiedeman arriving in 1812. Mark's grandparents settled in Indiana in 1917.

Tilly started dating Mark in high school. After graduating from Harvard Law School, he'd done a stint in a high-powered law firm in Los Angeles, but had returned to Caruthers Corners with wife Tilly and their daughter Agnes. Now they had three more, Taylor and Mandy and little Whatzername. Almost more children than she could handle.

The four children needed a big house to roam around in. So did Tilly. The mansion could hold everybody – like a castle.

Hadn't Tilly's mother always said she was a princess in training?

CHAPTER THIRTY-TWO

The Old History Teacher

The National Guard still had the town under lockdown. Trucks continued bringing in bottled water and MRE's and donated clothing. Nearby towns were contributing vegetables and other produce. Old MacDonald's was giving away free milk and butter. The congregation of Peaceful Meadows raised $32,412 for needy families.

A number of people had left town, off to stay with relatives or out-of-town friends. Several others were assigned FEMA trailers. 132 moved back into damaged homes. But 532 remained in the Red Cross shelters.

Doctors were offering free medical exams. Shrinks from Burpyville Memorial were providing grief counseling.

Mayor Mark Tidemore had set up a command center at the Town Hall to coordinate all of the activities. Chief Purdue loaned him Myrtle Dobbler to orchestrate it. Myrtle was good at her job – like a juggler, but with voice messages instead of rubber balls.

~ ~ ~

That next afternoon Cookie returned to volunteering at the Red Cross food tent, handing out bottled water and MRE's – today, franks and beans – to the hoards staying at the mass shelter.

Glancing up, Cookie caught sight of a familiar figure. She took a second look to make sure. The hunched man with the shiny dome had to be her old history teacher, Justin Ford Harribald. Even living in the same small town, she'd rarely seen him since high school. Maybe an occasional wave across the aisles at Food Lion.

"Mr. Harribald – Justin – is that you?" she called into the milling crowd.

The elderly man turned at the sound of his name. She was surprised at how much he'd aged. But, of course, he had to be at least 75 now. She only been 17 when she was his student – his teacher's pet, as her classmates teased. That was over 40 years ago!

"Hello there," he squinted. "Is that you, Katherine?"

"Yes, it's me. I'm glad to see you survived the twister."

"Takes more than that to kill an old cuss like me."

"How have you been?"

"Retired for more years than I can remember. It's boring as heck."

"You're looking well," she lied. When she'd been his student he'd looked something like Wallace Shawn, that character actor from *The Princess Bride*. Now he looked more like a prune, wrinkled and leathery.

"You're as pretty as ever. I remember when you were Homecoming Queen."

"A long time ago," Cookie said. She'd been an A+ student in History, her photographic memory allowing her to memorize all the textbooks. Easy peasy lemon squeezy. She wondered if that was why he'd liked her so much, her interest in history. Or maybe the old devil flirted with all his female students.

"I follow your career with the Historical Society. You're my one student who actually found a use for what I taught."

"You should come visit our new digs. The Historical Society takes up a wing of the Perricock Museum. I'll give you a personal tour."

"I might take you up on that if life ever returns to normal."

She looked past the crowd, at the devastation in the distance. Roofless houses. Broken telephone poles and single walls of buildings. Piles of rubble. Overturned cars. A virtual Armageddon. "It will ... one of these days," she said.

"I've also followed your adventures as a crime solver. What do they call you girls – the Quilters Club?"

"Oh that. My quilting group gets carried away from time to time. Thinking that we're Miss Marple, Jessica Fletcher, Kay Scarpetta, and Kinsey Milhone all rolled into one."

"But you've solved a few crimes."

"I suppose we have."

"Then I have a clue for you. I saw the person who broke into your friend Elizabeth's quilting museum. I was going to report it to the police, but the aftermath of this tornado has been so chaotic."

That got Cookie attention. "You saw the man who pried open the door?"

"No, I saw the girl coming out with a big quilt over her arm. I don't know her name but I'd recognize her if I saw her again. Blonde, pretty. She reminded me of that movie star – what's her name? – Missy Montana. I saw her in that movie, the remake of *10*. The girl who robbed the museum could've passed as her sister."

"How did you happen to see this girl stealing a quilt?"

"What's that phrase I remember you used to say – easy peasy? I live just across the street from the quilting museum. I sit at my window every Tuesday and watch you come there with your friends. Of all my girls, you were my favorite."

CHAPTER THIRTY-THREE

Septuagenarian Stalker

"Hey, guess who I bumped into," said Cookie. Today was Tuesday and the Quilters Club had gathered as usual at the Hoople Quilting Heritage Museum – no matter that the town lay in rubble around them. Tradition was tradition.

"Who?" replied Lizzie. "One of the missing monkeys?"

"Hardly," said Cookie. "Ben and Bombay found the three monkeys late yesterday afternoon. They were hanging out in an abandoned house on Melon Rind Road."

"So who did you run into?" asked Lizzie. Taking the bait. She was distracted with a complicated stitch. French knots were tricky.

"I bumped into our old history teacher."

"Justin Harribald?" said Maddy. "Is he still alive?"

"Not only is he alive, but he lives across the street."

"From where?" said Lizzie, looking up.

"Here. Across the street from here."

"Get out!" said Lizzie. "Justin Harribald lives across from the quilting museum and we didn't know it?"

"Yeah. It was kinda creepy. He said he watches us come and go every Tuesday. He's probably watching the front door right now."

"That sounds like a stalker," commented Aggie, concentrating on her stippling, a meandering free-motion quilting stitch that never crosses itself. She was getting pretty good at it.

"He probably is a stalker," chuckled her grandmother. "Mr. Harribald always had a thing for your Aunt Cookie."

"Ugh! A teacher putting the moves on a student!" said Aggie. But her indignation made her think of Mr. Griffith, always talking trash to her from behind the door of his locker every morning. Asking if she had a boyfriend? Did she like older men? What would she be willing to do to have an acting career? Truth is, she found it flattering.

"He was so smart and knowledgeable back then," said Cookie. "But now he's just ... old."

"You're not a spring chicken yourself," Bootsie pointed out. While Bootsie had always been pudgy, her friend Cookie once had been slender and limber, head girl on the cheerleading squad. No wonder Mr. Harribald had taken her under his wing, the old lecher. Of course, that was before Cookie started dating BMOCs like Bob Brown and Ben Bentley – husbands number one and two.

"Thank you for those inspiring words," sniffed Cookie. "But Justin had something interesting to tell me."

"That you flunked history but he gave you an A anyway?" laughed Maddy.

"Hey, I got an A+ if you remember. I believe you girls squeaked by with C's and B's."

"Guilty as charged," admitted Bootsie. "But it was a C+." Emphasizing the plus.

Cookie smiled. "I'll give you that."

"So what info did your old, uh, mentor have to tell you?"

"That he saw the break-in. Well, the tail-end of it."

Lizzie looked up. Green eyes flashing like a burglar alarm coming to life. "He saw the person who stole the Marie Webster?"

"Yes! He said it was a blonde girl. That she looked like that movie star, Missy Montana."

"Ha!" said Bootsie. "What would a movie star be doing in this little town?"

~ ~ ~

Justin Harribald had taught both American History and European History at Caruthers High. Despite the world population argument, the School Board saw no need of a course in Asian History, although that had been Mr. Harribald's major in college.

An unkissed frog, Justin Harribald had never married. Instead he carried on with various students over the years, a firing offense these days, but pointedly overlooked forty years ago. He was particularly fond of cheerleaders. Going out for the squad used to be referred to among the students as "trying out for Mr. Harribald's team" – although he'd had nothing to do with the Athletics Department.

His biggest scandal had been a double dalliance with the Simpson sisters, twins. His longest "protégé relationship" was with Bitsy Johnson, throughout her senior year and after graduation, right up until the time she married Sherman Smoot. But out of all his girls, Katherine Svenson – Cookie, to her friends – had been his favorite.

Afterward, he had followed her life from afar, from when she married Bob Brown, to later when she married Ben Bentley. And he was so proud when she began working as the Town Historian, climbing the ladder to Executive Director of the Caruthers Corners Historical Society, and merging it under the roof of the Perricock Museum of History and Science.

~ ~ ~

That evening as Cookie was leaving the quilting museum, she glanced at the line of houses across the street. Lower-middleclass clapboard structures, not quite shabby. She wondered which one Justin Harribald lived in. Oh well, no matter.

Best hurry, she told herself. It was 6:30. Curfew in half an hour.

But as Cookie walked toward her car, something caught her eye: the movement of a curtain in the window of that gray house directly across from the museum's entrance. She could feel she was being watched.

CHAPTER THIRTY-FOUR

The Scoop

Lucius Plancus had got the assignment to look into the murder because Kenny Kincaid turned up zip. Now he was about to suffer the same fate, embarrassment that he'd lobbied for a story that had just hit a dead-end. The perp had been released from jail, disappearing into the chaos of a town in the midst of a natural disaster. Nowhere to be found. End of story. Thirty, as the newspaper guys say.

But as Plancus stepped out of the police station, he'd noted a sign in the window of Cozy Café that advertised: WATERMELON MILKSHAKES! HOT COFFEE! ICE COLD LEMONADE!

Lemonade! What was that old saying? *If they hand you lemons, make lemonade.*

There might be a way of turning the story around, doing a profile on a man who got away with murder. A dead film professor. An actor called Robert De Niro. A disgraced lawyer pulling off a legal Hail Mary. Yes, he could turn this into a fine glass of lemonade.

All he had to do was locate Robert De Niro. Or was it Robert Di Nero?

Never mind. That new deputy had let it slip that the FBI's fingerprint database identified the alleged murderer as Robert Dietrich Black.

That gave him something to work with.

For only $19.95, an Internet site called FindYourMan.com told him that Robert Dietrich Black's last known address was on East Street in Indianapolis, only a few blocks from the Lockerbie Square Historic District, where Hoosier poet James Whitcomb Riley once lived.

Maybe Lucius Plancus would climb into his rusty '94 Oldsmobile Cutlass Supreme, the last Olds convertible ever made, and drive down to Indy and knock on Mr. Black's door. Just to see who answered.

~ ~ ~

The East Street apartment was a second-floor walk-up. There was no buzzer but the front door was unlocked. Lucius Plancus squeezed his girth up the narrow stairwell and banged on the door of 2A. There were only two apartments on the second floor, A and B. So he figured he had a fifty-fifty chance with 2A.

"Who's there?" came a growl.

"Pizza delivery."

The door swung open. "I didn't order any pizza," said the square-faced man wearing a tattered bathrobe over boxer shorts and a white V-necked T-shirt. The apartment behind him looked like a rat's nest, fast-food wrappers cluttering the dirty floor, lampshades askew, stuffing spilling from the couch's brown cushions like a gutted hippopotamus.

Plancus stuck his big foot into the door jam, preventing the door from being closed. The six locks on the thick metal door might keep burglars out, but once opened there was no closing it with the reporter's Size 13EE shoe blocking the way.

"Are you Robert Black?"

"Hey, what is this? Are you some kind of salesman?"

"I'm Lucius Plancus with WZUR." He had his palm-sized digital recorder running. "Are you the Robert Black who was accused of shooting a teacher at Caruthers Corners High this week?"

"Get out of here," the man tried to slam the door. But it wouldn't budge with Plancus' foot in the jam. "I'll call the police."

"Go ahead. That's your right," said the oversized redhead. "In the meantime, I have a few questions."

"You can't harass me. A judge let me off. There are no charges against me for shooting that rotten tyrant."

Plancus realized he'd got a break. The story had been lost amid the bigger news about the deadly tornado. No other journalists had bothered to track Black down. Or maybe they were still looking for a Robert De Niro.

"You shouted 'Death to tyrants!' when you shot Martin Lorenzo Griffith. What did you mean by that?"

"He stole my credit, that selfish autocrat. I co-directed that picture."

"Beg pardon?"

"He stole my director's credit. Only listed me as an actor. Me and Marty and Lloyd co-wrote the screenplay, put together the money, and co-directed it. I deserve credit. And my share of the money."

"What money?"

"Never mind that. He robbed me of my director's credit."

"But you did get credit for starring in the film, right?"

"Sure, me and Missy Montana had the leads. But Marty and Lloyd had major roles too. It was a low-budget film. Everybody did everything. Act, handle the sound, lighting, you name it. The financing came from a bunch of wealthy dentists who wanted to tell people they were movie producers. Most of it went for hiring Missy Montana. She was the big-name draw. Half the production budget was to pay for her."

Lucius Plancus looked confused. "That's why you shot Martin Lorenzo Griffith – because he didn't give you proper credit for co-directing the film?"

"Sure, I shot him. I don't mind admitting it, because they can't charge me again. Double jeopardy and all that. The Fifth Amendment to the Constitution states that no person shall 'for the same offense to be twice put in jeopardy of life or limb.'"

"That doesn't mean –"

"Hey, I know my rights. I've got a good lawyer. I walked on that murder charge, didn't I?"

"Why did having your name on the film as co-director matter so much?" persisted the reporter. "All the reviews said *Three Weddings and a Funeral* was a stinker."

"I could have saved the film if Marty had let me edit it. But no, he had to be the big man, run everything, boss us around, hog all the credit, control all the money – a tyrant!"

"So you shot him."

"You bet I did. Now leave me alone. I'd shoot you too, if I still had my gun. I killed Marty Griffith and I'd do it again."

There, thought Lucius Plancus, I have his confession on tape – a real scoop!

CHAPTER THIRTY-FIVE

N'yen's Brainstorm

The Quilters Club didn't have a chance to touch base that next day. Maddy was busy, dealing with Hoosier State Casualty and Property re her homeowner's claim. Cookie was volunteering at the Red Cross. Bootsie was tied up at the animal shelter (the iguana had escaped). And Lizzie was having a meltdown over the stolen Marie Webster quilt.

Aggie felt abandoned. The Quilters Club had pretty much given up on pursuing the murderer of Martin Lorenzo Griffith – partly because of a lack of leads, partly because their attention had been diverted by the theft of that stupid ol' historical quilt.

Even Uncle Jim and his deputies had been sidetracked by that darned twister.

Nobody seemed to care that Robert Di Nero A/K/A Robert Black was free, the charges against him seemingly dropped.

Would he kill again?

The answer to that would likely be found in why he shot Marty Griffith at point-blank range in front of a dozen witnesses. Surely, there was more to it than a childish pique over a directing credit on a bad film. Sane people didn't murder people over a stupid movie, did they?

According to the Rotten Tomatoes website, 67 noted film critics hated the movie, certifying it as

Rotten. But she hadn't seen Peter Travers or Rex Reed or A.O. Scott stalking around her school with a handgun.

Maybe her friend Prissy was right: Life has to go on.

Aggie simply had to accept that justice isn't always served. Robert Black was going to get away with murder and there was nothing she could do about it.

~ ~ ~

Marybelle Olsen came with impeccable credentials. British by birth, she had worked for a member of the Royal Family before emigrating to America. When the Duke of Whatever passed away – he'd been hit by a lorry crossing Trafalgar Square – Marybelle had decided to try her fortunes in the New World.

A well-regarded placement agency in New York had matched her skills with Miss Hilda Hoople, and off she went to Indiana.

Indian Territory indeed, she'd already met a genuine redskin at the Dollar General Store. This Indigenous American by the name of Matea Davis had helped her locate a tea strainer among the hodgepodge of kitchen gadgets displayed on a far wall of the store.

Miss Hilda enjoyed high tea. It was a civilized custom that Marybelle hoped to introduce to the manse's guests. Miss Tilly was very receptive to new practices. And the girl – Agnes – she showed promise too.

Miss Maddy was a strange sort, the leader of a sewing bee, a group of women who fancied themselves to be latter-day Sherlocks. Always solving crimes, according to local tittle-tattle. She hoped they were cerebral about it. She wouldn't abide with gun battles in the billiard room or fistfights in the foyer.

The girl – the older one, not the three smaller terrors – professed to be a member in training of the Quilters Club – for that's what this sewing bee was called. Chasing criminals sounded like a dangerous pursuit for a pubescent teenager. However, young Agnes tended to emulate her grandmother, rather than her own mum. What was that saying about traits skipping a generation?

~ ~ ~

That night N'yen Madison phoned his cousin. Phone service had been fully restored and Aggie had good reception at the Hoople Mansion. She could see the new cell tower from her bedroom window. Emergency crews had erected it literally overnight.

"I've been thinking about that missing Marie Webster quilt," he said. Their Aunt Lizzie had not yet reported the stolen "Pink Dogwoods in Appliqué" to the Indianapolis Museum of Art.

"Any ideas? We're at a dead end."

"I thought you said you guys had narrowed the suspects down to Faith Ann Ritchie."

"True. She's both a customer of Helen of Troy Spa and a Crackleton with a family full of thieves to help her steal the quilt."

"Then what's the problem?"

"Margie Yost says Faith Ann hasn't had a hair appointment with her in six months. So she couldn't have heard about the Marie Webster quilt. Aunt Lizzie only told Margie about it last week."

"I see what you mean by dead end."

"You're the brainiac. Do you have any bright ideas?"

"Just one."

"What's that? Or do I have to say pretty please?"

"That wouldn't hurt."

"Okay, pretty please. With sugar on it."

"There might be a simpler answer – you know, Occam's razor."

"Simpler? Like what?"

"I was in the Badger Patrol with Buddy Smyth. His mom is Margie Yost's sister. Margie might have told her."

"But Patricia Smyth wasn't on Margie's customer list."

"You don't have to be a customer to talk with your sister."

CHAPTER THIRTY-SIX

Maddy's Distraction

For the past few days Maddy had been dealing with insurance companies and buying new wardrobes for the family and replacing little things like toothpaste, razors, and aspirin. Electricity at the old address had to be turned off. Water and garbage service cancelled. Milk delivery diverted. Mail forwarded.

Same for Tilly's household. Plus, Aggie needed a new computer, school clothes, you name it. And Tige was out of dog food.

On top of that, both families needed new cars. Insurance would cover the replacement of their automobiles, but that required a ton of paperwork. Maddy's big Toyota Sequoia had been found, a piece of twisted metal at the foot of High Jinks Hill. Beau's old Buick had been sitting in the garage of their house at the time of the tornado. It probably still was – wherever the garage might be. Tilly and Mark's brand-new 2018 Mercedes Sprinter low-roof passenger van had left only a side mirror behind as proof that they'd ever owned it.

Meanwhile, Lizzie and the other members of the Quilters Club – their homes having been spared – continued to pursue the thief who took the "Pink Dogwoods in Appliqué."

Today the three women gathered at the Red Cross tent where Cookie was volunteering. Taking a break, she pointed them to a vacant folding table and brought over some MRE boxes – chicken nuggets and peas. Nearby there was an urn of dark sludge-like coffee, along with a cannister of powdered creamer. And plastic bottles of water were stacked on an adjacent table.

"Sorry I'm late," said Aggie, sliding onto the bench beside her friends.

"We just got here," replied Bootsie, reaching for a box of chicken nuggets. Aggie could smell the greasy delights from across the table.

"We haven't started talking about the quilt yet," nodded Cookie, taking a Styrofoam box for herself.

"We've just got to get it back," Lizzie moaned. The redhead was worried sick over the missing quilt. She pushed her MRE box away. For the past two days he'd quit eating, her way of dealing with stress. She looked all the more skinny.

"Let's think it through," urged Cookie, the logical one of the group. She stirred her coffee with a flat wooden stick before taking a sip. She made a face at the taste. But what the heck – it was free.

"What about Justin Harribald's claim that he saw a woman come out of the museum with the quilt?" asked Bootsie.

"That's just plain silly," said Lizzie. "He said she looked like that movie star, Missy Montana." She had looked Missy up on IMDb but there wasn't much listed there. A horror flick called *Monster Massacre* was cited as her first film. That remake of *10* got her noticed. But *The Winter Storm* had been her big breakthrough. Then she nearly sank her career with that trashy *Three Weddings and a Funeral*. She had a new film called

The Sexy Single Girl in the works. IMDb described its status as being in Pre-Production.

Now that was an interesting coincidence, that Missy Montana had starred in a movie directed by that dead film teacher. However, nobody knew what to make of it. Synchronicity, perhaps.

"Okay," admitted Cookie. "Maybe Mr. Harribald is getting a bit senile. He's in his seventies, for goodness sake."

"What would a movie star be doing here in Caruthers Corners?" laughed Bootsie. "That's ridiculous."

~ ~ ~

They sat there sipping on the mud-like coffee. Wishing they were at Cozy Café where the java was better. For only 50-cents, you got an "endless cup" of good-to-the-last-drop Maxwell House – caffeinated nectar of the gods, in Cookie's opinion.

Aggie passed along N'yen's tip about Margie Yost's sister, but the members of Quilters Club weren't quite sure what to do with that either.

"I know Patricia Smyth," said Lizzie. "She belongs to the macramé group that meets at the Hoosier State Senior Recreational Center. Patty might be a little odd, but I can't quite see her as a thief."

"Me either," agreed Bootsie. "Those macramé types aren't interested in quilts, even rare Marie Webster appliqués. They only think in terms of rope and string and twine – silly crafting materials like that."

"Patty Smyth's also a devoted mother," said Cookie. Her foster son Gus had been having play dates with Buddy Smyth. He seemed like a nice kid from a nice home.

"Besides, she doesn't look a bit like that movie star," Lizzie added. Patricia Smyth had a long horsey face that reminded you of Sarah Jessica Parker. Missy Montana was more the Charlize Theron type.

"What about Patty's husband? Would he help her steal a quilt?" asked Bootsie.

"Donald's manager of the Dollar General," Lizzie pointed out. "He's also president of the Rotary. Why would he risk all that?"

"I hear he's a bit of a lady's man," said Cookie. Offering a lecherous wink, deliberately tweaking her friend Lizzie. She could tell the redhead had a bit of a crush on him.

"Oh, Donnie's flirty," admitted Lizzie. "Always coming on to his female customers. But he's harmless."

"Do you know this first-hand?" Cookie couldn't imagine her friend stooping to shop at a lowly Dollar General without an ulterior motive. Lizzie's tastes were too upscale for a bargain store.

"Oh, I admit I've stopped by the Dollar General from time to time. It's a handy place to pick up nail polish remover." The redhead changed shades of fingernail polish the way other women changed dresses.

"Are you saying Donald Smyth came onto you?" pressed Cookie.

"Why would you find that surprising? I keep pretty fit. He's only a few years younger than me."

"Maybe if you count in dog years," muttered Bootsie under her breath. Donald Smyth was in his mid-40s. Lizzie had just turned 60.

"What was that you said?"

"Nothing. Just clearing my throat," replied the pudgy brunette. Pretending to examine the chicken nuggets in her foam food box. They were cold.

"Let's chat with Margie Yost about her sister and brother-in-law," suggested Lizzie. "But we'd best be circumspect. If we falsely accuse her family members, I'll never get another hair appointment at Helen of Troy ever again."

~ ~ ~

Beau Madison took over negotiations with the insurance company regarding the house on Melon Pickers Row. Or the lack of house.

As the former owner of an Ace Hardware, he knew something about construction. Rebuilding a home was a complicated project, but he could talk the language – at least enough to not let the insurance adjuster take shortcuts in the appraisal of damage. Their home would have to be rebuilt from the ground up. A contractor had just given him an estimate of $284,691.

Maddy had been eager to rebuild, but after meeting with Hilda Hoople and Barnabas Soltairé, she'd backed off a bit. Something was up, Beau suspected. After nearly 40 years of marriage, he could read his wife pretty well.

He wondered if she had decided they were ready for a condo. Or a senior living community. But that seemed unlikely. They were both still pretty vital. No need to pack it in to that degree. Or was he reading it wrong?

Maddy wasn't talking. She seemed preoccupied with Tilly and Aggie. They were enjoying the change of pace, living in a large rambling house with multiple bedrooms, a formal dining room, well-stocked library, hidden passageways, two elevators, twelve fireplaces, a walk-in freezer, and even a small bowling alley.

Hilda Hoople's new factotum, Marybelle Olsen, served as caretaker, maid, cook, laundress, and the old woman's companion. Quite the cook, Marybelle made the best roast beef with watermelon sauce that Beau had ever tasted. And she turned down the beds every night, placing a mint on the pillow, just like at a hotel.

Easy to get used to.

Aunt Hilda flitted around the mansion like an unvanquished ghost. Happy to have the company, she chattered and giggled and told stories of the Hoople Quadruples as children, tales that entertained them one and all.

Tilly was delighted to have discovered a new branch of the family. Aggie viewed the woman as an ersatz fairy godmother. Her little sisters ran through the hallways like a band of marauding Indians. Tige joined them, barking like a junior-sized coyote. Mark was never there, supervising the town's recovery.

Maddy smiled and nodded, content to be in the bosom of her new family. Beau was pleased to see his wife so happy.

But, exhibiting uncanny prescience, Aggie worried that danger still lurked on the periphery of their lives. She dreamed of a shadowy figure stalking her from room to room throughout the mansion. What did that forebode?

PART IV

"You are welcome, most noble Sorceress, to the land of the Munchkins. We are so grateful to you for having killed the Wicked Witch of the East, and for setting our people free from bondage."

- L. Frank Baum,
The Wonderful Wizard of Oz

CHAPTER THIRTY-SEVEN

With a Lead Pipe

Lloyd Frankenheimer was found bludgeoned to death in his apartment in Carmel, a suburb just north of Indianapolis. A lead pipe lay in a pool of blood next to his body. Nobody doubted that Robert Black had done the deed. A message spray-painted on the wall declared: *DEATH TO TYRANTS!*

The Federal Bureau of Investigation was called in, this beginning to look like the work of a serial killer. The FBI defines serial killing as "a series of two or more murders, committed as separate events, usually, but not always, by one offender acting alone." A serial killer is neither a mass murderer, nor a spree killer.

Technically, Robert Black didn't quite fit any of the above descriptions. He appeared to be some sort of psychologically aberrant revenge killer.

Needless to say, this made Chilly Willy LaMont fearful that he might be next in line. The police in Caruthers Corners hadn't been very helpful. So he'd requested the FBI's protection, but they referred him to the Indy police. The Indianapolis PD declined to provide personal protection but agreed to have a cruiser do a drive-by every three or four hours.

That wasn't good enough for the talent agent, so he checked the Yellow Pages and called a firm listed as Iron Fist Enterprises. It offered "bodyguards, surveillance, and security," according to an ad in the lower righthand corner of the page. The listing featured the black-and-white image of a Ninja warrior.

After a quick phone call with Iron Fist's director – a man with the unlikely name of Drake Hammer – he had a security agent assigned to him 24/7 until further notice. It was costly, but Chilly Willy knew Bobby Black would be coming for him next.

~ ~ ~

Police Chief Jim Purdue received a BOLO from the FBI for one Robert Dietrich Black, A/K/A Bobby Black, A/K/A Robert Di Nero, A/K/A Robert De Niro. But the Chief had no reason to think Bobby Black would be headed this way again. Other than the late Martin Lorenzo Griffith, there was no local connection to the killer or his flop of a movie.

Or so Chief Purdue thought.

At that very moment, Louise Carol König rolled into town to visit her widowed mother and estranged sister. She hadn't been home in five years, ever since setting off for Hollywood to become a movie star. But she'd been in Indy on a publicity tour when the tornado hit, that catastrophe raising concerns about her family's well-being.

Hollywood hadn't happened right away, so early-on Louise had supplemented her income as a stripper, a career choice that cut her off from her ultra-religious family. Of course, that brief period of her life didn't show up on the studio's biography.

Right now she was under contract with Bad Bunny Productions for a film based on the life of Helen Gurley Brown. She was lucky to get anything, following *Three Weddings and a Funeral*. But Wilson LaMont was a determined agent, burning up the phone lines, working hard to get her career – and his – back on track.

Five years ago LaMont had signed Louise König straight out of high school, got her a few Little Theater roles in Indy, then funded her move to Hollywood. He was that sure she was star material. He'd even supplemented her income when she was stripping. Then came her role in the remake of *10*. That put her on the map. However, her breakthrough role was Elsa in *The Winter Storm*. *Hollywood Reporter* called her performance "mesmerizing." *Variety* declared: "Give us more of Missy Montana." *Entertainment Weekly* listed the film as A+ and added, "Where has Hollywood been hiding Missy Montana?"

Then came that awful indie film *Three Weddings and a Funeral*. It was supposed to be a parody of the 1994 British comedy with Hugh Grant and Andie MacDowell. But nobody got the joke. To make matters worse, there was all that legal business, the lawsuit that halted the film's theatrical run. Maybe that was for the best, given the bad reviews.

Fortunately, Wilson LaMont had managed to come up with the lead role in the Helen Gurley Brown biopic. That had been a lifesaver!

Louise owed a lot to LaMont. The agent had even given her the stage name of Missy Montana. That was funny. She'd never even been to Montana.

CHAPTER THIRTY-EIGHT

Time to Leave

Bobby Black had tried to be reasonable with Lloyd Frankenheimer, but Lloyd claimed no knowledge of the $200 grand. So he'd dispatched him just as he had Marty. Two down, two to go.

Bobby was determined to find that money. He'd killed Marty and Lloyd for not talking and he intended to keep on killing people till someone cracked. He had no compunction about whacking Missy or Chilly Willy if they refused to turn over the loot.

He could practically smell that money, he was getting so close. One of them had it – he was sure of that!

Onward! Death to tyrants.

~ ~ ~

Odell Lumley had been taken aback by the death of Lloyd Frankenheimer. No question Robert Dietrich Black was behind it. He was obviously on a killing spree.

Was the private eye himself at risk? Probably not. Black was after that fabled $200,000, and Lumley had no knowledge of its whereabouts. His investigation had turned up zip.

Black would strike again, the PI suspected. But who would be the target? Another member of the film crew? The cinematographer? The producer? The best boy? The script girl? His co-star?

It was like playing spin the bottle.

Then Lumley asked himself, What if Black thought the PI had actually found the money and kept it all for himself. That wouldn't be good. He could wind up just as dead as Griffith and Frankenheimer.

Hmm.

Maybe now would be a good time to take a little vacation to the Bahamas.

~ ~ ~

The missing iguana turned up in Birdie Longstreet's backyard. She thought it was a dinosaur. "Help! There's a Tyrannosaurus Rex sitting in my grandson's wading pool. Can you send animal control?"

Myrtle Dobbler took the 911 call. "You're saying there's a T-Rex in your wading pool?"

"That's right! A reptile about eight or ten feet long, I'd say. Got spikes along its back. A big waddle under its neck. Covered in gray scales. Long claws that are about to poke a hole in my grandson's pink blowup pool."

"Stay away from it," said Myrtle. "I'll send somebody out right away."

She caught Petie Hitzer in his cruiser about three blocks from Birdie Longstreet's house. "Birdie says it's a dinosaur," repeated the dispatcher. "Ten feet long."

The deputy's chuckle reverberated over the police radio channel. "Shucks, that sounds like Ol' Horace, the iguana that escaped from the animal shelter. I'd say he's maybe four-feet from nose to tip of his tail."

"That being the case, try not to shoot him or else you'll be facing the wraith of the Chief's wife. Mizz

Bootsie likes that oversized lizard. She feeds him flowers."

"Don't worry. I'll bring Horace back to the animal shelter safe and sound. I'm more worried about Birdie. She's liable to have a stroke."

"Birdie sure sounded like she was about to pop a vein when she called 911."

"Hope this don't keep her from showing up at church on Sunday. She leads the choir, you know." Petie and his family were longtime members of St. Paul's. The Hitzers were devout Methodists.

~ ~ ~

Aggie was on her way to the weekly Quilters Club meeting. The sewing bee wanted to get back to familiar routines. Tuesday was the day they always got together to work on quilting projects.

In olden days, quilts were a practical bed covering made of padding enclosed between layers of fabric and kept in place by lines of stitching. Its purpose was to keep sleepers warm at night. But the fabric bedspreads had morphed into an art form with the decorative stitching and creative designs.

In addition to bedding, modern quilts are used as wall hangings, table runners, and tablecloths. Quilt shows and competitions are held locally, regionally, and nationally. The Quilters Club's members always entered the annual Watermelon Days competition. Aggie had won prizes in the junior category. Lizzie was a champion, winning year after year.

The hike from the Hoople Mansion to the quilting museum where they met was about two miles, but Aggie was in good shape, limber and agile from her gymnastic training. She was on the high school team. The girl was adept at the balance beam, flips, and vaulting horse.

National Guardsmen were still visible, helping with the cleanup. Piles of refuse lined the streets, awaiting pickup. It would be hauled to a dump site down near Pitsville.

She saw Thelma Ann König coming down the street. Thelma Ann was dressed to the nines. A far cry from the plain smock she'd worn while serving soft serve ice cream – custard, they called it locally – at the Dairy Queen.

Aggie was sure going to miss the DQ. A weekly ritual, she and her dad went for Blizzards every Wednesday afternoon. She was particularly fond of mint Blizzards, although the watermelon flavor was pretty good too.

Why did Thelma Ann look so happy? You'd think she'd be sad, out of a job. Only a cement slab to mark the spot where the DQ once stood.

Thelma Ann had a smile on her face and a spring to her step. Her blue dress hugged her curves. She looked like a woman in love.

Aggie recognized the signs. She felt that way sometimes about Bobby Elwood. But who was Thelma Ann dating? Hadn't she broke up with Buddy Flynn?

Well, Caruthers Corners was a small town. Word would get out soon.

CHAPTER THIRTY-NINE

The Sister

Being a movie buff, Maddy had often remarked that the star of *The Winter Storm* reminded her of one of the König girls. It was natural to notice lookalikes. She wondered what had become of that oldest girl – what was her name, Louise? Hadn't she left town? Gone off to college? Took a job in Indy? She couldn't recall.

The younger sister – Thelma Ann, that was *her* name – worked at the DQ. Well, she had prior to the tornado. The Dairy Queen along with its concrete picnic tables had been blown away to who knows where.

It had been a bad storm.

The Town Square's Ferris wheel ended up in N.L. Purdue's living room, destroying a third of his house with its spaceship-like landing. That was the least of N.L.'s worries. His chair factory suffered major damage. Half of the E-Z Seat building had been reduced to woodchips.

Everybody had a story: Aggie's bicycle wound up on Fourth Avenue, twisted into knots like a metal pretzel. The shoes of Sad Sammy's cousin were found a mile from his dead body. A delicate Hummel figurine belonging to Mrs. Elsie Warton had landed on a neighbor's cement patio without suffering a single chip. Mrs. Francine Jenkins was still trying to figure out how to get her silver Honda Civic Si out of a tree on South Main.

Later that day, Maddy noticed Thelma Ann König working the cash register at the Dollar General. The girl had bounced back really fast, already finding a new job. Maddy had stopped by the discount store to pick up a few more personal items – deodorant, toothpaste, shampoo, etc. It was aggravating to have to replace *every*thing.

While she was at the Dollar General, Maddy made a point of waving hello to Matea Davis. The young Native American liked having a day job, particularly one as unpressured as stocking shelves. It gave him free time for his new role as Troop Leader of the Badger Patrol. The search and rescue activities winding down, he was back on the job. All the missing townspeople had been accounted for.

While Maddy was there at the store, she also paid her respects to Donald Smyth. Her grandson N'yen had been in the Badger Patrol with the manager's son Buddy. The boys had liked each other, as she recalled.

"You're looking particularly lovely today," Smyth complimented her. A tiny bit obsequious. Maddy recalled Don's reputation as a lady's man, but perhaps she was being overly sensitive.

Or maybe not.

Because he took her hand, like a gentleman about to plant a kiss on top. He held it a little too long. She caught Thelma Ann König giving them a dirty look. Either disapproval or jealousy, she couldn't tell which. It made her feel uncomfortable.

~ ~ ~

On the way home, Maddy swung by the Hoople Quilting Heritage Museum, hoping to catch the tail-end of the Quilters Club gathering. It was already Tuesday again. She lost track of days under this artificial existence of a demolished town, displaced citizens, and National Guard patrols. She wasn't used to living with a curfew.

Only 4:30 p.m., her friends' cars were still there in the graveled parking lot, so she pulled her rented Mitsubishi Mirage into a slot and pushed her way past the turnstile at the front door. She noticed that the broken lock had been replaced with one twice as large. Security after the cow had left the barn, she thought to herself.

"Hi all," she called out as she entered the sewing room where everybody was stitching away at respective patchwork quilts. Their National Quilting Day project had been set aside. No Guinness Book of World Records awards coming anytime soon.

Today Lizzie was working on a Postage Stamp quilt, assembled entirely of 1" fabric squares, sewn together in parallel rows. Very time consuming, but Lizzie was the fastest sewer among them.

Cookie was struggling with a traditional Flying Geese pattern. Flying Geese are comprised of rectangular patchwork quilting components twice as long as they are tall, each with a peaked triangle at its center. Small triangles flank opposite ends of the peak. The design is reminiscent of the V formation you see with flying geese during the fall.

Bootsie was doing a Jelly Roll quilt, one of the easiest patterns to master. The Jelly Roll fabric is precut into long 2 ½"-wide strips and you can use a simple sewing method to put it together. Most quilters can do one in a half-hour to forty-five minutes. Two hours if you're Bootsie.

Aggie was working on a Star quilt, a gift for her friend Matea Davis. Star patterns gained popularity among Native Americans in the late 19th Century. They have a spiritual and cultural importance for many tribes.

Maddy gathered up her fabric scraps and sat down in her regular chair. She was doing an Amish quilt pattern called Streak of Lightning. Its construction was simple. Corners are butted, rather than mitered. Midwestern Amish quilts also feature narrower borders to balance the fancier piecing.

"Any progress on the missing Marie Webster?" asked Maddy as she began stitching one block to another to create the basic lightning design.

"We're down to one suspect," said Aggie. "N'yen came up with the idea."

"But it's pretty weak," admitted Lizzie.

"Somebody other than Faith Ann?"

"We had to eliminate her," said Bootsie. "She hadn't been to Helen of Troy lately. So Margie Yost couldn't have told her about the quilt."

"Who then?"

"Donald Smyth. His wife is Margie Yost's sister. Margie could have told her."

"Hmm, I'd forgotten Donnie's wife was Margie's sister," said Maddy.

"Remember, Margie told us that when we got our facials."

"Patricia Smyth fits our theory," Aggie pointed out. "If the leak of information came from Margie Yost."

"Where else?" said Lizzie. "I've been wracking my brain, but I can't think of anyone else I told."

"How did N'yen figure out the connection?"

"He knows the Smyth's son Buddy," said Aggie. "From the Badger Patrol."

"I should have caught it," sighed Cookie. She knew all the genealogies in the county, but Margie Yost lived across the line in Burpyville.

"Donald and Patty as burglars," mused Maddy. "I'm not sure I buy it. That would be like Ken and Barbie turning into the Hamburglar."

"I admit it's a stretch," said Lizzie. Showing doubt. "But we've run out of suspects."

"They deserve a close look," countered Cookie. "We don't know that much about Donald Smyth. He's from out of town." A touch of Xenophobia in her tone.

"Where did Donald come from?" asked Maddy.

"Don Smyth grew up in Terre Haute," confirmed Cookie. "He met Patricia Yost at Indiana State University. They got married, settled down in Terre Haute, and had a kid. They lived over there until moving here about a year ago."

"He looks kind of thuggish with that broken nose," observed Bootsie. Something of a believer in physiognomy when it came down to it. She considered herself proficient at judging a person's personality by their physical appearance.

Maddie raised one eyebrow. "He probably got that broken nose playing football at Indiana State."

"Margie says he got it from an angry husband," confided Lizzie. "That's why they left town, to make a fresh start here in Caruthers Corners."

"That's right," nodded Bootsie. "Margie said her brother-in-law was quite a Lothario. She said he even made a pass at her, his own sister-in-law."

"I find that hard to believe," said Lizzie. "I can't believe Donnie would be attracted to all that green hair."

"Margie's hair changes colors like a kaleidoscope," Cookie reminded her friend. "Last month it was pink."

"True," Lizzie admitted.

"Did you think Donnie only liked redheads?" teased Bootsie.

"Oh you," Lizzie swatted at her friend with a fat quarter.

"Ladies, you're getting carried away. I saw Donald Smyth not twenty minutes ago," remarked Maddy. She unconsciously fluffed her silvery hair. "He said I looked lovely today."

"Um-huh," Bootsie rolled her eyes.

"It was all very innocent. But I noticed Thelma Ann König giving us a disapproving look."

That seemed to catch Lizzie by surprise. "Thelma Ann? She's the Dairy Queen girl. What was she doing there?"

"Working there, I think. She was running the cash register at the checkout counter."

"What happened to Brenda Sprunger?" Cookie wanted to know. "She's been the head cashier for as long as I can remember."

"Beats me," said Maddy. "Maybe she had the day off. Thelma Ann could be the relief shift."

"Now that's quite a match," laughed Lizzie.

"What do you mean?" asked Bootsie.

"Don Smyth and Thelma Ann König – I'm not sure who's the bigger flirt. She practically seduced Edgar every time we went by the DQ for a Dilly Bar."

"Edgar?" said Cookie.

"Why not? He's kinda handsome in a rugged way."

"Your husband is old enough to be her grandfather."

"Tell that to the little tart," said Lizzie. Showing a flash of jealousy for the first time that any of her friends could recall. "I think Thelma Ann has Daddy Issues."

CHAPTER FORTY

An Irreplaceable Artifact

The recovery of the "Pink Dogwoods in Appliqué" quilt was paramount on the Quilters Club's agenda. Its loss would be a blight on Lizzie Ridenour's reputation in the quilting world ... and on the future of the Hoople Quilting Heritage Museum.

Even worse would be the loss of an irreplaceable American artifact. In Lizzie's opinion, it was like someone stealing Da Vinci's *La Joconde* or Botticelli's *Primavera*.

As America's first quilting celebrity, Marie Webster is credited with quietly reviving the art of quilt making in the early 1900s. "Pink Dogwoods in Appliqué" is considered a significant work by Webster. And her "Grapes and Vines" had been selected as one of *America's 100 Best Quilts of the 20th Century.*

At the time, women were accustomed to sewing almost all of their clothes, bedding, and household goods. Webster offered a fresh perspective on using quilts in the home. Her design principals reflected the Colonial Revival style, the lines in Art Nouveau work, and the sensibility of the Arts and Craft Movement.

In 1909, she broke with traditional Victorian quilt patterns and created her first appliqué quilt. She worked in pastels, showing that the dull predictability of the Victorian era was over. Her original designs changed the look of American quilts forever.

Appliqué – or "laid-on" quilts – usually has a top made of whole cloth with smaller pieces of contrasting fabrics cut into shapes or forms that are applied or stitched down.

The term for this ornamental style of needlework comes from the Latin word *applicō* meaning "I apply" and subsequently from the French *appliquer,* which means "to cover" or "put on."

Back then, appliqué quilts were considered more elegant than "the humble pieced type." But they also provided a new creative challenge for American women. Particularly women who longed for a more modern decor.

Typically Webster's designs included a center medallion composed of flowers and strong borders. Medallion quilts feature a central motif surrounded by multiple borders. The style offered endless possibilities for quilters.

Marie Webster wrote in 1915, "City women, surrounded by many enticing distractions, are turning more and more to patchwork as a fascinating yet nerve-soothing occupation."

"The Colonial Revival brought back a *desire* to make quilts, not the *necessity*," notes historian Kimberly Wulfert. "Women had less time to spend on needlecrafts now, making kits and patterns ever more popular with the masses."

Thus Marie Webster had both things going for her, an appealing new sense of design, plus a kit-approach to quilt making – a winning combination.

~ ~ ~

N'yen's idea that Donald Smyth and his wife might be behind the theft of the Marie Webster quilt was hard for Lizzie to accept. Patricia Smyth belonged to the Garden Club. Everybody said she was a good mother. Donald was head of the Rotary Club, had just been invited to join the Lion's Clubs, and was a member of Toastmasters International.

Model citizens by all reports.

Lizzie liked Donnie Smyth. He was so very friendly. Always complimenting her on her hair (Thank you, Margie Yost), admiring her outfits, flirting with her. She was flattered. When you became a "lady of a certain age," you took sweet talk wherever you could get it.

Surely, if he were behind the missing quilt, he wouldn't be able to look her in the eye. She wanted to see for herself, so she marched down to the Dollar General store after the Quilters Club meeting to check out Donnie's demeanor. She would look him straight in his eyes and see if he flinched. Like being a human lie detector.

"Hi, Missus Ridenour," he greeted her. "I heard you and Edgar escaped the twister."

"Yes, it didn't come anywhere near us out there on the river."

"Patty and I came through okay too. Missed our house. And Buddy was in school. Everybody safe."

"Thank goodness it missed Dollar General. I see you're doing a steady business."

"Yes, but we're almost out of inventory. All the food stuff has sold out. Tools and such pretty much gone. I may have some nail polish left, if you've come to stock up."

"Uh, yes. That's why I'm here."

"Your nails look lovely." He took her hand to inspect her fingertips. "You've had them done recently."

"Yes, your sister-in-law painted them just last week."

A voice interrupted them. "Hello, Mrs. Ridenour. Nice to see you."

Lizzie turned to spot Thelma Ann König. She'd almost forgotten that Maddy mentioned the girl was working here. "Oh, hello, Thelma Ann.

"How is your husband?"

"Edgar's fine, thank you."

"Guess I won't be selling him any more Dilly bars for a while."

Lizzie could feel her blood pressure rising. "I saw that the Dairy Queen's gone. Are you working here now?"

"Yes, Donnie was nice enough to offer me a job."

Lizzie looked around as if searching for someone. "What happened to Barbara Sprunger?"

Donald Smyth gave her a smile wider than a Cadillac's front bumper. "Oh, Barb's taking the week off to visit her sister. She wanted to get away from all the tornado destruction. It was so upsetting to her. Thelma Ann will cover for her, give us more flexibility in shifts."

"Is your wife Patty going to stay here, or go back to Terre Haute until this mess gets cleaned up?"

"I think she may go visit her sister Margie over in Burpyville. They're pretty close, you know."

Like a spider, she sprung her trap. "Did Margie happen to mention my upcoming Marie Webster quilt exhibit?"

"She might have. But I don't pay much attention to that kinda stuff. Women's business, you know."

Lizzie looked him directly in his blue eyes, but he didn't flinch.

CHAPTER FORTY-ONE

A New Home

"Pooh Bear, can we talk?"

Beau looked up from the newspaper. He liked to skim the *Burpyville Gazette* over breakfast. Marybelle had prepared pancakes this morning. "What is it, dear?"

Mark had already gone to work, early bird that he was. Tilly and Aggie had joined them for pancakes. The little kids were still in bed. Aunt Hilda was taking poached eggs in her room as usual.

"We don't have to rebuild our house on Melon Pickers Row, unless you really want to."

"I'm not sure what you mean," he replied, looking puzzled. "Are you saying you want to buy a condo?"

"Not exactly. Aunt Hilda has made us a generous offer, if we choose to accept it. She's invited us to live here permanently. Tilly and her family too."

"In the mansion?"

"Yes, right here atop Hoople Hill. She's leaving the house to us in her will. But in the meantime both families are free to take over a wing – one for us, one for Tilly and Mark."

"What about me?" Aggie spoke up.

Tilly said, "You'd get your own suite in our wing. Each of you girls would have a separate room. Wouldn't that be nice?"

Beau glanced at his daughter. "Looks like both of you are in on this. Am I the last to know?"

"Kinda. We haven't told Aggie's sisters yet. Not that they get a vote."

"Do I get a vote?"

"Yes, of course, Pooh Bear. You get the deciding vote," said Maddy, carefully sipping her coffee. It wasn't as good as Cozy Café's Maxwell House, but not bad. Marybelle was quite a find.

"What about Mark?" He valued his son-law's opinion. Mark the Shark was one smart cookie, in his opinion. "What does Mark have to say about this idea?"

Milly smiled shyly. "Mark says it's up to you. He'd be happy to stay here if you agree."

"And you?"

"Dad, you know I've always fantasized about this big old place. I've always wanted to live in a castle."

He turned to Maddy. "You too?"

"This house will belong to us one day. Aunt Hilda wants to keep it in the family. Maisie gets Wabash Acres. She's happy with that."

"Hmm, which wing do we call home?"

"Your choice, Dad," said Tilly. "Mark's never home. And I'd be happy anywhere within these stone walls, princess that I am."

Aggie blurted, "I want my room as far away from my pesky sisters as possible." The Trio of Trouble, she called them. It had been so much nicer when she was an only child.

"Maybe we'll put you in the basement," teased her mother. "I'm sure there a dungeon down there somewhere."

"Aw, mom."

"Hmm, a wing for each of us," mused Beau Madison. The mansion's floorplan was laid out like a cross. Each wing offered the privacy of a town house.

"Aunt Hilda already has her own wing. Then one for us, one for Tilly's family, and the fourth wing reserved for guests."

"Are we expecting guests?"

"Bill and Kathy will come visit. And we'll set aside a room for N'yen," proposed Maddy. "His permanent home away from home."

Beau liked that idea.

CHAPTER FORTY-TWO

Getting a Bodyguard

Chilly Willy LaMont liked his new bodyguard, a guy named Rex Blouderman. His boss referred to him as Agent X-3, as if he were a black ops combatant out of a paperback thriller. Blouderman was big and beefy, the physique you wanted in a bodyguard. He wore silvered sunglasses and carried a Taser that gave off 50,000 volts of electricity. Needless to say, he dressed in black cargo pants with many pockets and a black tee that advertised IRON FIST SECURITY in bold blood-red letters.

Rex Blouderman sat behind the wheel of a black BMW parked across the street from Chilly Willy's modest ranch house in Poplar Grove, a neighborhood about 7 miles southeast of downtown Indianapolis. Agent X-3's Steiner MM1050 Military-Marine 10 x 50 binoculars rested on the passenger seat within easy reach. The speaker for a portable security alert ("I've fallen and I can't get up") was mounted on the SUV's padded dashboard. All his client had to do was press the red button on the device that hung on a lanyard around his neck and X-3 could be across the street in less than 20 seconds – ready to intervene with any threat.

~ ~ ~

Chilly Willy regretted that he had put Missy Montana in for the lead in Martin Lorenzo Griffith's film, *Three Weddings and a Funeral.* At the time it sounded legit. The filmmakers had financing, a decent script – what they needed with a "name." After *10* and *The Winter Storm*, Missy had a certain cachet. Bankable, as they say in Tinsel Town. He got her a better-than-scale deal.

He'd signed Missy as a client the day after she turned eighteen. He saw something in her pretty blonde looks and bubbly demeanor that seemed salable. Star material. Had he harbored carnal thoughts about her? Probably, but he'd never acted on them. Over the years, she became more like a surrogate daughter, with him supplementing her income out of his own pocket – like an allowance. Now with this Helen Gurley Brown film, his investment would finally be paying off. The money was very good on this one, seven figures. Her first time breaking the million-dollar mark.

In two weeks Missy had to report to Toronto where Bad Bunny Productions would be filming the biopic – a cheap substitute for New York City. That lookalike locale – plus tax credits – locked in Canada as the site for the project.

In the meantime she had decided to go visit her family over in Caruthers Corners. She hadn't been home in five years. Her ultra-religious mother had cut off all communications after Missy – Louise, as he mother still called her – got to Los Angeles. "Whore of Babylon," her mother had shouted before hanging up the phone for the last time. Missy had muttered, "But I'm in Hollywood, not Babylon."

Betty Lou König was a staunch member of Salvation Baptist church. Known as Primitive Baptists, its members believed that wearing lipstick or a red dress was a ticket straight to Hell. Louise failed on that criterion along with many others.

Chilly Willy tried to dissuade his client from this visit home, knowing it would not end well. However, Missy was worried about her mom and sister after that terrible tornado plowed through the little Indiana town. She was determined to check on them. Maybe she also had a secret agenda to make amends with her family.

Missy's sister was the wild card. Never close while growing up, the two siblings remained at odds even today. Thelma Ann resented her sister's success, blaming Louise for leaving her behind to work at a Dairy Queen while she flitted from glitzy film festivals to wild yacht parties to red-carpet movie premieres, hobnobbing with the likes of Tom Cruise and Bradley Cooper and Ryan Gosling.

Truth was, Missy Montana had never met any of those big-name stars. She was set to co-star in the Helen Gurley Brown pic with Jeffrey Tambor, but she hadn't even met him yet. Nobody had ever heard of her co-star in *10*. She'd played opposite George Carnard in *The Winter Storm*, but he'd been a jerk with bad breath and a drinking problem.

Fact is, the role of Helen Gurley Brown was not as glamorous as one might think. The late *Cosmopolitan* editor was famous for writing *Sex and the Single Girl*. But in real life, she was married to dapper-but-dull movie producer David Brown of *Jaws* fame. No single life for Helen – a challenge for the film's scriptwriters.

The New York Times had described the Cosmo Girl as "self-made, sexual and supremely ambitious ... she looked great, wore fabulous clothes and had an unabashedly good time when those clothes came off." Well, Helen Gurley Brown was certainly ambitious and self-made.

So was Missy Montana. Maybe that's why the casting directors gave her that part. She wore her ambition on her sleeve like a corsage.

Chilly Willy tried to get a message to Missy, but she wasn't answering her iPhone. Probably hadn't paid her bill this month. He needed to warn her about Bobby Black. The guy had gone off his nut. Killing people!

Marty and Lloyd were dead. He knew he and Missy had to be on that wackjob's to-do list. That was scary.

~ ~ ~

Lucius Plancus enjoyed a nice exclusive with his on-the-spot interview with the accused killer, Robert Dietrich Black. Yet the story of a 28-year-old actor freed on a Writ of Habeas Corpus didn't "have legs." However, that changed instantly when the FBI was called in following a second death, that of the screenwriter of *Three Weddings and a Funeral*.

With the death of Lloyd Frankenheimer Bobby Black had made it onto the FBI's Most Wanted list. Now *that* was a story ...

... and the big redheaded reporter had a head start on it.

Back at WZUR, Plancus replayed his digital recording, picking out new passages to include in his next broadcast. Lots of good stuff here. He'd kept Black talking for quite a while. The guy had been a motormouth.

Black was under the misassumption that he couldn't be charged with the murder of Martin Lorenzo Griffith, that somehow the habeas corpus would create Double Jeopardy. Even a layman like Plancus knew better than that. Double jeopardy only exists when there has been a previous *final* judicial decision.

Black's habeas corpus was a non-final judgment. Being no verdict was reached, Black had not been placed into jeopardy, thus the Double Jeopardy Clause of the Fifth Amendment did not "attach."

The jerk should get a better lawyer.

Lucius Plancus had recorded Black's verbal confession to the murder of Griffith. That would be a biggie. He might just get a job offer from an Indianapolis station. Indy was the largest radio market in the state. With 1,542,800 Metro 12+ listeners, it ranked number 39 out of 268 in the entire USA.

But before he could air the confession, Bobby Black had struck again.

CHAPTER FORTY-THREE

Danger, Danger

The suburban ranch-style house of Wilson "Chilly Willy" LaMont wasn't very fancy for the digs of a big-time movie agent, Bobby Black thought as he cased the joint. The paint on the trim was peeling. One shutter hung at an angle. A few shingles were missing from the roof.

The grassy backyard was blocked off with a high chain-link fence. No easy access there. The side windows had thick bars. Nix them too. Best approach would be straight in the front door, he decided.

Bobby crossed the street and marched up the cobble-stone walkway like a Jehovah's Witness on a mission from God. Instead of a handful of *Watchtower* pamphlets, he carried a snub-nose .38 revolver.

Without glancing around, he began pounding on the wooden front door. "Open up," he yelled. "I want my money."

No sound from inside the house.

But down the street in the black SUV a red light flashed and the mobile security device on the dash emitted a *beep! beep!*

Immediately, Rex Blouderman was out the car and running toward the house like a greyhound out the gate. "Hold it there!" he shouted to the shadowy figure standing at the front door.

The intruder turned and pointed an object at Blouderman. The security man saw a flash and felt a fist hit him in the chest. He went down as if he'd just run into a brick wall. *Umph!*

He wasn't even sure he'd heard the sound of the gun.

Not waiting to assess the damage, Bobby Black turned and sprinted toward an old Nissan parked up the street. As Blouderman regained his senses, he heard a car start and drive away with a whining screech of tires. The guy was escaping.

Blouderman sat up and gingerly felt his chest. Sore! Fortunately, Agent X-3 of Iron Fist Security had been wearing his Point Blank Level IIIA body armor, a polyethylene bulletproof vest capable of stopping bullets with a velocity exceeding 2,000 fps. The impact of the .38 slug had left a purplish welt on his breastbone. It hurt like a son-of-a-gun. But he was alive.

"Is he gone?" called Chilly Willy from the doorway.

"Definitely gone," grunted Rex Blouderman. "But I'm calling headquarter for authorization to use deadly force. This is getting life-and-death serious." He had a Glock G31 in the gun safe bolted to the back floorboard of his SUV. Time to get it out.

"I've been telling you guys my life was in danger," said Chilly Willy.

"Yeah, but now *mine* is in danger too. I'd be dead without the vest."

Just last week Blouderman had scored 380 with his pistol at the Iron Fist gun range. Equivalent to an

Expert rating in the US Marine Corps. Agent X-3 was angry and ready for a fire fight.

Nobody shot an Iron Fist agent and got away with it, he told himself. A hollow-point .357 round would easily stop Robert Black if he returned for a second try.

CHAPTER FORTY-FOUR

Prodigal Daughter

Missy Montana knocked on the door of the white clapboard house on Jinks Lane. The same rundown bungalow in the same Blue Collar neighborhood where she grew up. However, the surroundings now looked surreal, one side of the street a normal middleclass Ozzie-and-Harriet neighborhood, the other side like a Syrian landscape strewn with rubble and the broken walls of collapsed buildings.

"Who is it?" came a raspy smoker's voice.

"It's me – Louise."

"Who?"

"Your daughter Louise."

Pause. "I don't have a daughter named Louise."

Missy stamped her foot. "Open the door, Mom. Your Prodigal Daughter has come home. At least for an hour or two."

Silence.

"Mom?"

Silence.

Missy sighed. "Where's Thelma Ann?" she shouted at the door.

"At work."

"Is she still at the DQ?"

"Twister blew it away. She's got a new job at the Dollar Store."

"I'll be back later," she called to her mother.

"Don't hurry."

~ ~ ~

Missy found Thelma Ann behind the checkout counter at the Dollar General. The unexpected appearance caught Thelma Ann by surprise: "Louise, what are you doing here?"

"Just dropped by for a visit. But Mom wouldn't let me in the house."

"Do you blame her, the way you left us?"

"Left you? I went into the world to make my way. Nobody told you to stay here."

"I like it here. This is a nice town."

"Then why did you get so angry because I didn't send for you? You haven't spoken to me in five years, baby sister."

"You could have sent some money home. You were living high on the hog, while I was stuck here on Jinks Lane."

"Ha," laughed Missy. "You finally got the bedroom all to yourself. You always hated sharing it with me."

"Well, I don't need you now, big sister. I'm going to be rich myself."

"And how are you going to do that, pray tell?"

"My boyfriend and I came across an article of great value. We're going to sell it to a private collector. Then I'll be moving out to a fancy house of my own."

"Boyfriend? Are you still seeing Buddy Flynn, the guy who owns that Texaco station out on Highway 21?"

"No, I've done much better than that. My boyfriend happens to be –"

"Hello there," interrupted a voice. "Is this your sister Louise?"

Missy turned to see a tall handsome man with a nose that was slightly askew. "I go by Missy these days. And you are –?"

"– Donald Smyth. Smyth with a *y*. I'm the manager of this Dollar General." He offered a wide piano-keys smile. "I must say you are even more lovely in person than you appear on the screen. I've seen all your movies. You were simply magnificent in *The Winter Storm*."

"Donnie, nobody is supposed to know my sister is Missy Montana," hissed the blonde checkout clerk

"But you told me –"

"In secret."

"Oh."

"You're saying nobody in town knows I became a movie star?" Missy looked as if about to cry. Her lower lip quivered. She blinked back tears.

"Mom said it was our shame. You know she never approved of your career choices. Especially when you worked as a stripper."

"A what?" said Donald Smyth.

"– a dancer," corrected Missy.

"A stripper," her sister insisted.

"I worked temporarily as an ecdysiast to research a film role," she replied coolly. Giving Thelma Ann the ol' Evil Eye.

"I must've missed that one," said Smyth. "I'd sure like to see it." He eyed her curvy body as if he had X-ray vision.

"Donnie, cut that out. I'm your girlfriend, not her."

"It's all in the family," he winked. "You two look a lot alike."

"You think so?"

"Being that she's your sister I'd sure like to get to know Louise – I mean Missy – better."

"You stay away from her, buster. I'm the one who knows that collector who's willing to buy that Marie Webster quilt. You can't sell it without me."

Donald Smyth looked around nervously. "Careful what you say," he hissed. "Somebody will hear you."

But there were no customers in the store. Word was out that Dollar General was low on inventory. Customers had shifted to Home Depot.

"What quilt?" said Missy.

"Never mind," sniffed her sister. "Welcome home."

CHAPTER FORTY-FIVE

Gun Play

Bobby Black pulled the .38 from underneath his loose flannel shirt and checked the cylinder. It was fully loaded, five shots in all. He'd found the revolver in a drawer at Lloyd Frankenheimer's apartment after he whacked him on the head with a lead pipe. The police hadn't returned the gun he'd used on Marty, but this one would do just fine.

He was convinced that the hoity-toity movie star had been in cahoots with Marty and Lloyd. After all, the four of them – himself included – had the same agent, Wilson LaMont. They had ganged up on him, like a bunch of tyrants, stripping him of a co-directing credit on *Three Weddings and a Funeral*. He needed that to get into the Director's Guild. His big step toward a Hollywood career. They had cheated him of his future and deserved to die – all of them.

And then there was that not-so-small matter of the money – $200,000 missing, according to the dentists. Now that was a lot of teeth cleaning.

He wanted his share. No, that wasn't true. He wanted all of it.

He'd read in the *Indianapolis Star* that Missy Montana was in town for a publicity tour. Her studio was already promoting *The Winter Storm* for an Oscar. Buzz had it she might get a nomination herself for the role of Elsa, the young Russian seamstress who helped stave off the German attack on Moscow. Following the old Russian saying that there is no such thing as cold weather, only the wrong kind of clothing, Elsa had helped dress the Russian troops for a winter war against the ill-clad Nazi invaders. The film was being promoted as "a moving romance set amidst the heart-chilling battles of World War II."

Bobby had located Missy at Le Méridien International, the historic hotel formerly known as the Canterbury. When she checked out the next morning, he tailed her rental car in his non-descript '06 Nissan. She headed northeast, passing through Burpyville, then taking Highway 101 – the main road, not the bypass – toward Caruthers Corners.

He was puzzled why she would be heading toward this small out-of-the-way town, traveling without her usual entourage. The studio publicity tour included a handler – talent escort, they called the position – and two PR assistants, their job being to shuttle Missy from interview to interview. The day before she had talked with the *Indianapolis Star*, *Southside Times*, WTTV-TV Channel 4, WTHR-TV Channel 13, and WXLW Talk Radio. A busy schedule.

Bobby followed her to a small white house on Jinks Lane, and then downtown to the Dollar General store. He watched her go inside, looking sleek and sensual in a blue Herve Leger bandage sheath dress. Through the large plate-glass window (newly replaced), he watched as she had an animated conversation with a blonde girl at the checkout counter. Then they were joined by a tall man with an Owen Wilson nose. Nobody else entered the store, so he decided it was time to act. He exited his parked Nissan and strode purposely across the street, entering the store by its main entrance.

"Hello, Missy," he said, pointing the snub-nosed .38 at her unblemished forehead. He'd always admired her porcelain-smooth skin. It was going to be a shame to mar it.

~ ~ ~

Aggie and her Dad had a weekly ritual of going for Blizzards at the Dairy Queen every Wednesday afternoon. Now that the DQ was gone, they had to make do. So they agreed to get a couple of Klondike ice cream sandwiches at the Dollar General.

As they stepped into the discount store, something seemed amiss. There were four people gathered at the checkout counter: Thelma Ann König stood behind the cash register, the manager next to her. A familiar-looking blonde waited in front of the counter, with a square-faced man positioned a few feet away. They seemed startled by Aggie and her dad's sudden appearance, freezing like players caught in a game of Spotlight.

"Hi, Thelma Ann," Aggie greeted the girl who usually sold her DQ Blizzards. "What are you doing behind the counter?"

"I-I work here now."

"Hello, Don," said her dad. "How are you doing today?"

The manager glanced nervously at the other man, then mumbled, "J-just fine."

The blonde customer caught Mark Tidemore's attention. He said, "Say, aren't you –?"

"Yes, I am."

"What are you doing in our little town?"

"Actually, I'm from here," she replied.

"This is my sister," Thelma Ann offered.

"Missy Montana's from Caruthers Corners and no one knew?" Mayor Mark Tidemore was aghast. "Surely your classmates or neighbors would have recognized you up there on the big screen."

"Hiding in plain sight. Nobody expects to see Louise Carol König in a movie."

Aggie spoke up. "My Grammy always said you reminded her of a local girl."

"And she was right," nodded the movie star. "Everybody comes from somewhere."

Aggie shifted her attention to the square-faced fellow who seemed to be standing in line at the checkout counter. "And I recognize you. You're the man who shot my teacher. I saw you do it."

"What?" said her dad, taking a step back.

Bobby Black pulled the .38 snub-nose from under his floppy shirt. "You're a very observant little girl."

"I'm almost sixteen," she said, kind of a *non sequitur*.

"I'm here to deliver death to tyrants," he declared.

"Hey, I'm no tyrant," proclaimed Donald Smyth. "I'm a fair boss. I gave Barbara Sprunger the week off ... with pay."

Bobby Black frowned at the store manager. "Not you, you idiot. Missy here. She helped them rob me of my film credit."

"I did no such thing," protested the blonde. "I was a hired actor just like you."

"I wasn't just an actor. I was the co-director too."

"Really?" said Missy. "I don't recall you directing any of that stupid movie. Maybe if you had, it wouldn't have been such a bomb. *Three Weddings and a Funeral* almost destroyed my career."

"It did destroy mine. I can't get a job as an actor or director."

Aggie spoke up. "Maybe you should change your name. Who came up with Robert De Niro anyway? That was already taken."

The man looked offended. "That's just a stupid nickname Marty and Lloyd gave me back in college. I kept it as a stage name."

The girl cocked her head quizzically. "So what's your real name?"

"Robert Black. My ancestors were Scottish, not Italian."

"There goes your chance to star in a *Godfather* remake," the girl said flippantly.

"Andy Garcia wasn't Italian."

"No, but Brando, De Niro, Pacino, Pesci, Liotta — all those guys are Italian Americans."

"Robert Anthony De Niro Jr. is only part Italian on his father's side. His mother was of Dutch, English, French, and German ancestry."

"How can that be? He starred as Don Corleone in *Godfather II*. And as a gangster in *Goodfellas*."

"He played one in *Casino* too. But that doesn't make him a Sicilian mobster. He's an actor, for goodness sakes. Just like me."

"Ha!" said Missy Montana. "Not according to the critics."

"Hey, watch it. I don't want to do a *Godfather* remake anyway. I'm looking for an original screenplay to option. No more lousy remakes for me."

Aggie said, "I thought *Three Weddings and a Funeral* was supposed to be a prequel, not a remake."

"Whatever," he waved her words away.

The man turned his attention back toward Missy Montana. "Do you have it?"

"Have what?" Missy looked puzzled.

"You know, the money."

"What money?"

Aggie spoke up. "Killing Marty and the scriptwriter hasn't been about film credit, it's about money."

"What money," Missy repeated.

"The money Marty hid in a film cannister," Aggie replied.

Bobby Black's eyes lit up. "You know where it is?"

"Yes, as a matter of fact, I do."

"Give it to me or I'll kill you too!"

"No," said Aggie, "I don't think so."

In his frenzied state, Bobby wasn't aware that she had been deliberately distracting him while Matea Davies eased up behind him with an Indian's stealth. The stock boy had been working in the back of the store this whole time, overhearing the murmur of conversation at the cash register.

"Drop your gun or I'll shoot," growled Matea in his best Matt Dillon voice. He'd grown up watching *Gunsmoke* as a kid on the rez. When playing cowboys and Indians, he'd always been tapped to be a cowboy.

"W-what –?" Bobby turned to see the young Potawatomi pointing a serious-looking pistol at him.

"Drop that gun. I'm not going to ask you twice."

Bobby released the Charter Arms Undercover Special, letting the snub-nose revolver clatter to the linoleum floor. "Wait! Don't shoot," he begged, raising his hands over his head.

Mark Tidemore scooped up the .38 and pointed it at Bobby Black. "Aggie, go next door to the police station and get your Uncle Jim. Tell him Matea just captured a murderer."

"I'm not a murderer," Bobby insisted. "I'm an avenger!"

"And I am a *memegwesi*," said the Native American. "I protect children."

Aggie smiled. "Thanks, Matea. I'm glad you made me and N'yen your Blood Brothers."

"It is my honor, *nikan*."

"Where did you get that big pistol?" she asked about the gun in his hand.

"Toys – Aisle Six. I had to remove the red tip on the barrel so it would look real."

CHAPTER FORTY-SIX

The Quilt Is Found

"**A**re you Quilters Club ladies missing a quilt?" asked Matea Davis at the Badger Patrol luncheon. That weekend the Sons of Anthony Wayne had thrown a big shindig to honor the Troop Leader for his bravery in capturing a murderer on the FBI's Most Wanted list. The young Potawatomi was taking an "Aw shucks" attitude to the tribute, pointing out that he'd just happened to be at the right place at the right time.

"Why do you ask?" Maddy replied cautiously. Lizzie had yet to inform the Indianapolis Museum of Art about the disappearance of "Pink Dogwoods in Appliqué."

"Something I overheard Thelma Ann say before that crazy killer came into the Dollar General."

"Oh?"

So he told her.

Maddy motioned for the other members of the Quilters Club to gather around. "Matea has something you'll want to hear," she beckoned. "It's about the quilt."

"The quilt?" said Bootsie.

"*The* quilt," Maddy repeated, emphasis on the first syllable.

"Oh," said Lizzie, eyes widening. Not only her reputation, but the museum itself was on the line with the missing Marie Webster.

Matea lowered his voice, as if imparting a deeply held secret. "Thelma Ann König said she and Donald Smyth had come across 'an article of great value.' I think they were talking about a quilt."

"Do tell," said Lizzie. Their investigation had come close to mark. Turns out, the thieves were not Donald Smyth and his wife – it was Donald and his girlfriend.

"Thank you for this information," Maddy gave the young man a peck on the cheek. "You just saved the quilting museum."

"Yes," he smiled weakly. "But I may have cost myself a job. If Donald Smyth gets arrested, they'll probably close down the Dollar General. You can't run a store without a manager."

~ ~ ~

Chief Jim Purdue served a search warrant on Betty Lou König, the mother of Thelma and Louise. He found the Marie Webster quilt neatly folded in Thelma's bedroom, stacked on the top shelf in her crowded closet. With only the one tiny clothes closet, Jim wondered how the two König girls had managed to share this room while growing up. No wonder they disliked each other.

Mrs. König professed no knowledge of the purloined quilt being in the house. Missy was quick to confirm that her sister had admitted to stealing it. Deputy Pete Hitzer took Thelma Ann and her boyfriend into custody.

"Anything you say may be held against you ..." Petie recited their Miranda rights.

"I've said too much already," Thelma Ann muttered under her breath.

She knew the jig was up.

The 1925 Marie Daugherty Webster "Pink Dogwoods in Appliqué" quilt quietly returned to the wall in the Hoople Quilting Heritage Museum and the exhibit's opening was rescheduled. The Indianapolis Museum of Art was none the wiser.

EPILOGUE

Robert Dietrich Black got a mandatory sentence of 65 years for each of the two murders, but they were to be served concurrently. At present he's incarcerated at Indiana State Prison at Michigan City. He tells fellow inmates that he directed the popular British comedy, *Four Weddings and a Funeral*. He claims that his professional name is Mike Newell, and that he's personal friends with Hugh Grant. Some prisoners in the yard trade him cigarettes to tell them stories about Andie MacDowell. The actress has a big fan club in Cell Block H.

His new attorney has appealed on grounds of insanity. In Indiana that comes under Indiana Code Title 35. Criminal Law and Procedure § 35-36-2-5. It states: "If a defendant who is found guilty but mentally ill at the time of the crime is committed to the department of correction, the defendant shall be further evaluated and then treated in such a manner as is psychiatrically indicated for the defendant's mental illness." Even if successful, it likely won't change his incarceration – other than shifting him to Pendleton Correctional Facility for psychiatric treatment.

Convicted of a Level 6 Felony, Thelma Ann König and Donald Smyth were sentenced to two years each, Thelma Ann at the Madison Correctional Facility, Donald at Plainfield. Donald's wife filed for divorce.

Thelma Ann sends Donald love notes. He doesn't respond.

J. Harold Wentworth eventually got disbarred. He now sells cars at Burpyville Motors. Judge John Lawrence Bristol was censored for his unwarranted Writ of Habeas Corpus. But it didn't faze the cantankerous old jurist. That's why he's known around the Burpyville courthouse as "Bust 'Em Out" Bristol.

Mortimer Remus retired from his job as resource officer at Caruthers High. He moved to Florida to live with his daughter.

The probate court awarded Barbara Jean Eckert – Martin Lorenzo Griffith's sister – the $200,000 discovered in a film canister in his school locker. The claim for the money by a group of Toledo dentists was turned down for lack of provenance.

~ ~ ~

Missy Montana did not get nominated for an Academy Award for her role in *The Winter Storm*, but the film did get a nod for Best Costumes. It didn't win, but the nomination caused a positive blip in box office receipts. Chilly Willy LaMont had negotiated a "Bonus Clause," so both he and Missy benefited from the increased ticket sales. They were going to be rich. Well, modestly so.

Lucius Plancus received a job offer from *The Indianapolis Star*. But he turned it down when WZUR upped his salary. He was a broadcast reporter at heart. He got his own program, On the Ground With Lucius Plancus.

In one of the most impressive career moves that anyone hereabouts could recall, Matea Davis got promoted from stock boy to store manager at the Dollar General, filling the opening left by Donald Smyth's sudden departure. Kudos to the Dollar General Corporation.

Aggie got a new Film Appreciation 101 teacher, a retired director named Clive Henry. One of his better-known movies was *Sullivan Unravels*. It won an Audience Award at Sundance and got picked up by Lionsgate. However, due to his reputation for going over budget, he couldn't find work in Hollywood, so he fell back on his original occupation, teaching high school. As it happened, he got fired after only two months at Caruthers High for fighting with Principal Pawley over renting camera equipment. Finances were tight this year following the 2018 Northeast Indiana Tornado.

Mark Tidemore was named Indiana Mayor of the Year for his handling of the storm disaster. Tilly was very proud of him. Maddy watched their four children so Tilly could attend the award ceremony with him at the Indiana Conference of Mayors (ICOM) in South Bend.

Thanks to the Hoople-funded Caruthers Corners Restoration Coalition and some generous state and federal grants, the little town was making a speedy recovery. The Red Cross shelters were quickly replaced by more FEMA trailers, creating a teaming RV park on a far corner of Ben Bentley's farm. A boom in home construction began restoring the town's quaint-tree shrouded streets to their picturesque charm. Magnificent Victorian-style houses sprung up like mushrooms. MacVics, people called them. The economy was taking off again. Mark the Shark was a sure-bet for reelection.

Maddy and her daughter's two families were settling in at the Hoople Mansion. As big as an apartment building, there proved to be plenty of space for all. No tripping over each other's feet, each family was ensconced in their separate wings. There was even a room set aside for N'yen's visits.

Beau and his pal Edgar spent more time fishing on the Wabash. Especially when the young Vietnamese boy came to visit his Grampy and Grammy. Aggie was jealous of all this male bonding, but she didn't bother writing a letter of complaint (as she was wont to do) to her idol, Ms. Gloria Steinem.

As it happened. Aggie was keeping pretty busy with Bobby Elwood. Upon turning sixteen, his dad had given him a car, an ancient oil-leaking Fiat Punto. Mark and Tilly agreed she could go to the movies without having another couple along. Risky business perhaps, but they regulated it with very strict timing. No dawdling after a movie let out.

~ ~ ~

The Quilters Club got back to sewing patchwork quilts. The Guinness Book of World Records was forgotten.

Lizzie had a great success with the exhibit of Marie Daugherty Webster's "Pink Dogwoods in Appliqué." The museum enjoyed a record attendance.

This opened the door for another big exhibit: A leftover panel from Mildred Potter Lissauer's famous Godey Quilt. This was a 1930s appliqué quilt composed of fifteen fabric portraits of men and women in fashionable mid-nineteenth century attire, an original design that wasn't representative of quilts of that era.

And in the process the Quilters Club uncovered a previously unknown textile dubbed The Frank Leslie Quilt, an appliqué design that predated the famous Godey Quilt by ten years or more. That was a mystery of historic significance – where did it come from? – at least to quiltmakers.

Even more startling was the fact that Maddy Madison's granddaughter Agnes discovered a hidden vault beneath the Hoople Mansion that contained an item that promised to rewrite the history of the town's famous quadruplets.

But that's a story told in the next Quilters Club book.

LIST OF CHARACTERS IN QUILT BLOCK

The Quilters Club
- Madelyn "Maddy" Madison, de facto head of the Quilters Club.
- Elizabeth "Lizzie" Ridenour, head of Hoople Quilting Heritage Museum.
- Katherine "Cookie" Bentley, head of Caruthers Corners Historical Society.
- Barbara "Bootsie" Purdue, head of animal shelter.

Quilters Club (Junior Members)
- Agnes "Aggie" Tidemore, Milly and Mark Tidemore's 15-year-old daughter. Maddy and Beau's granddaughter.
- N'yen Madison, Bill and Kathy Madison's adopted 13-year-old Vietnamese son.

The Husbands
- Beauregard Hollingsworth Madison IV, retired mayor.
- Edgar Ridenour, retired bank president.
- Ben Bentley, retired farmer, head of Sons of Anthony Wayne.
- Jim Purdue, Caruthers Corners Police Chief.

Maddy's Children

- Bill and Kathy Madison, oversee a children's shelter in Chicago. N'yen's adoptive parents.
- Freddie and Amanda Madison, local fire chief and his wife. Donna Ann's adoptive parents.
- Milly and Mark Tidemore, town's mayor and his wife. Parents of Aggie and her three younger sisters.

Maddy's Relatives

- Hilda Hoople, last surviving member of Hoople Quadruplets. Maddy's aunt.
- Maisie Walters, Maddy's separated-at-birth twin sister. Owner of Cozy Café.
- Sue Ann Polk, Maddy and Maisie's late mother.
- Emily Polk, Sue Ann Polk's sister.

Hoople Staff

- Barnabas Soltairé, former mob lawyer. Administrator of Hoople Quadruples Trust Fund.
- Marybelle Olsen, Hilda's new caretaker.

Aggie's Friends

- Robert "Bobby" Elwood, Aggie's boyfriend.
- Joan "Joanie" McPhee, Aggie's BFF.
- Pricilla "Prissy" Moretz, Aggie's BFF.
- Theodore "Teddy" DiMacchio, A/K/A Teddy D, Pricilla's boyfriend.

Pets

- Tige, Aggie's dog, a wire-haired Dachshund mix.
- Inka, Dinka, and Doo, Bootsie's three rescued dogs.
- Alexander the Great, Mrs. Warton's cat.

The Deputies

- Pete "Petie" Hitzer, police deputy. Parents own Old McDonald's Dairy.
- Tommy Truehart, police deputy. Lives with aunt.
- Myrtle Dobbler, police dispatcher. Elvina's sister.
- Elvina Dobbler, police dispatcher. Myrtle's sister.
- Mortimer "Morty" Remus, the high school resource officer.
- Evers Gochnauer, the late police chief.

The Tornado Victims (dead)

- Principal Fred Zwicky, Caruthers High School principal.
- Cromwell Thaddeus "Fatty" Johnson, carpenter. Former town Santa Claus.
- Maisie Daniels, mother of a former high school principal.
- Oliver Micherson, owner of Personally Yours flower shop.
- Jeff Brown, Oliver's life partner.
- Bob Norris "Big Nose" Evans, a local farmer and member of Town Council.

- Elsie Warton, widow of founder of Sons of Anthony Wayne.
- Seth Wagler, son of Abram Wagler, an Amish leader.
- Timmy Wertzel, son of Lionel Wertzel. A mechanic.
- Ivor Yokovich, an Azerbaijanian immigrant.
- Carlton Thomas, Matea Davis's across-the-hall neighbor.
- Rev. Benjamin Durrenberger, pastor of the First Mennonite Church.
- Rebecca Durrenberger, Rev. Durrenberger's wife.
- Martha Eldridge, an analyst at ZapData.
- Tom Accola, a shoe salesman.
- Samuel "Sam" Klondyke, manager at ZapData.
- Samantha "Sammy" Klondyke, Sam's wife.
- Stewart "Stewie" Klondyke, Sam and Samantha's son. Member of Badger Patrol.
- Floyd Hankins, cousin of Sad Sammy Hankins. Plus 18 others.

Badger Patrol

- Matea Davis, a Potawatomi Indian. Troop leader, works at Dollar General.
- Buddy Smyth, son of Donald and Patricia Smyth.
- Georgie Yager, son of Henry and Emily Yager.
- Bobby Bjorn, son of Roger and Elaine Bjorn.
- John "Kinky" Osbourn, son of Harvey and Ethel Osbourn.
  Plus 7 other Badger Patrol members.

Town Benefactors

- Bobby Ray Purdue, one of the Lost Boys. Second wealthiest person in town.
- N.L. Purdue, Bobby Ray Purdue's older brother. Owner of E-Z Seat factory.
- Boyd Aitkens, biggest watermelon farmer in the county.
  Plus Hilda Hoople, wealthiest person in town.

Various Townspeople

- Angela Pawley, the new principal of Caruthers High School.
- Donald Smyth, the manager of Dollar General. Head of Rotary Club.
- Patricia Smyth, Donald's wife. Member of Garden Club and macramé society.
- Thelma Ann König, worked at Dairy Queen.
- Louise Carol König, Thelma's big sister.
- Betty Lou König, Louise and Thelma Ann's mother.
- Justin Ford Harribald, a retired history teacher.
- Henry "Hank" Yager, a convicted murderer.
- Jasper Beanie, Town Hall custodian, cemetery caretaker, town drunk.
- "Fat Karl" Schaeffer, manager of Heirlooms Unlimited.
- Errol Baumgartner, a local farmer.
- Tim Mischler, a day laborer.
- Michael Allen Palley, an accountant.

- Mary Hegler, the town librarian.
- Hans Bitner, manager of Happy Times Mobile Home Park.
- Gabe Hilty, a barber. Owner of Snippets Inc.
- Ed Kensinger, manager at Food Lion supermarket.
- Donny Kensinger, son of Ed and Ethel Kensinger.
- Ed McGonigal, a self-employed day trader.
- Benjamin McPhee, Joanie's father. Retired. Chairman of annual Watermelon Days festival.
- Jerry Peach, analyst at ZapData.
- Fritz Berber, a local mailman.
- James Elwood, Bobby's dad. Manager at Home Depot.
- Sven Oberly, pre-med student and paramedic.
- Fritz Bruckhalter, night watchman at Industrial Park.
- Franklin D. Medford, MD, A/K/A Doc Medford, a physician and acting coroner.
- Brenda Sprunger, head cashier at Dollar General.
- Dr. Howard Carvel Oakman, curator at Perricock Museum of Science and History. Married to Smithy.
- Dr. Smithy Oakman, assistant curator at Perricock Museum of Science and History. Howie's wife.
- Darnell Watson, snow plower and street repair contractor.
- Arthur Adelphi, chair assembly foreman at E-Z Seat factory.
- Jean Simpson, a clerk at Home Depot. Sister of Jane Simpson.

- Jane Simpson, a clerk at Home Depot. Sister of Jean Simpson.
- Rita Rutaberger, an elderly widow living on an IBM pension.
- Andrew Linderman, produce manager at Food Lion.
- Emmanuel Linderman, Andrew's diaperless 2-year-old son.
- James Noah Kilroy, minister at Peaceful Meadows.
- Florence Kilroy, wife of the minister at Peaceful Meadows.
- Bitsy Smoot, a Sunday School teacher.
- Birdie Longstreet, sings in choir at St. Paul's United Methodist Church.
- Charlie Scherzinger, an ex-con who works at Grumman's Granary.
- Natalie Scherzinger, wife of Charlie Scherzinger.
- Roger Bjorn, an insurance agent.
- Elaine Bjorn, wife of Roger Bjorn.
- Harvey Osbourn, assistant manager of Home Depot's warehouse.
- Ethel Osbourn, wife of Harvey Osbourn.
- Sad Sammy Hankins, a watermelon farmer.
- Francine Jenkins, an Amway sales lady.
- Abram Wagler, head of a large Amish family.
- Ronald "Buddy" Flynn, owner of Flynn's Texaco.
- Lionel Wertzel, a mechanic.
- Clive Henry, a Film Appreciation teacher, director. Plus about 3,000 more residents.

Circus Folk

- Big Bill Haney, founder of Haney Bros. Zoo and Exotic Animals Refuge.
- Bombay Martinez, A/K/A Juan Martinez, manager of Haney Bros. Zoo.

The Media

- Lucius Plancus, reporter for WZUR.
- Kenny Kincaid reporter for WZUR.
- Jeffrey Snodgrass, weather reporter for WZUR.
- Clyde Carson, station manager for WZUR.
- Anderson Cooper, CNN anchor.
- John Powers Petrovitch, professional storm chaser.
- Stuart Frumkin, meteorologist.
- Oscar Zoroaster Phadrig Isaac Norman Henkle Emmannuel Ambroise Diggs Baum, a distant relative of L. Frank Baum.

Filmmakers and Associates

- Martin Lorenzo Griffith, Film Appreciation teacher, director.
- Robert Di Nero, actor.
- Lloyd Frankenheimer, screenwriter.
- Missy Montana, movie star.
- Wilson "Chilly Willy" LaMont, agent.
- A group of Toledo dentists, investors.
- Barbara Jean Eckert, Bobby Black's sister.

Hollywood Stars and Celebs

- Robert De Niro, actor in *Raging Bull* and *Taxi Driver*.
- Hugh Grant, actor in *Four Weddings and a Funeral*.
- Andie MacDowell, actress in *Four Weddings and a Funeral*.
- Danny DeVito, actor in *Get Shorty*.
- Dudley Moore, actor in *10*.
- Robert Towne, screenwriter of *Chinatown*.
- Wallace Shawn, actor in *The Princess Bride*.
- George Carnard, actor in *The Winter Storm*.
- Eric Longbottom, B-list actor.
- Ace Dobbs, B-list actor.
- Helen Gurley Brown, author of *Sex and the Single Girl*.

Film Critics

- Steven Rea of *The Philadelphia Inquirer*.
- Gene Siskel of *The Chicago Tribune*.
- Kenneth Turan of *The Los Angeles Times*.
- Thomas Elgort of *The Boston Standard*.
- Abe Coulson of *Chicago Herald-Standard*.
- Tom Dinsdale of *San Francisco Sexton*.
- Peter Travers of *The Village Voice*.
- Rex Reed of *The New York Observer*.
- A.O. Scott of *The New York Times*.
- Arthur Knight, author of *The Liveliest Art*.

The Crackletons

- Sarah Celine "Granny" Crackleton, matriarch of the Crackleton Clan.
- Ed Crackleton, Granny's younger brother. Father of numerous delinquents.
- Faith Ann Ritchie, Granny's daughter. Mother of Gus and several other kids.
- Augustus "Gus" Crackleton, Faith Ann's son. Cookie and Ben Bentley's foster son.

Legal

- J. Harold Wentworth, a shady lawyer from Burpyville.
- Judge John Lawrence Bristol, a corrupt jurist known as "Bust 'Em Out" Bristol.

Security

- Drake Hammer, head of Iron Fist Security.
- Rex Blouderman, Iron Fist Security's Agent X-3.
- Odell Lumley, a licensed Indianapolis Private Investigator.

Helen of Troy Spa

- Margaret "Margie" Yost, owner of hairstyling salon.
  Plus three hairstylists/aestheticians.

The Historic Quiltmaker

- Marie Daugherty Webster, famous appliqué quilter.

- Edward Bok, one-time editor of *Ladies' Home Journal*. A fan of the Arts and Crafts Movement.
- Kimberly Wulfert, a noted quilting historian.

Caruthers Corners Founding Fathers
- Col. Beauregard Hollingsworth Madison.
- Jacob Abernathy Caruthers.
- Ferdinand Aloysius Jinks.

END NOTES

Many of the quotes by tornado victims in this book have been appropriated from news accounts sharing the actual dialogue of real victims. This was done for the sense of verisimilitude. Names, of course, have been changed.

All tornado statistics found herein are accurate, to the best of my knowledge.

Thanks are extended to the National Weather Service, the Red Cross, the Indiana National Guard, and all other organizations referenced in this fictional telling of a natural disaster.

Marie Webster is a celebrated quilter and all references to her are factual.

- Marjory Sorrel Rockwell

Thank you for reading. Please review this book. Reviews help others find Absolutely Amazing eBooks and inspire us to keep providing these marvelous tales. If you would like to be put on our email list to receive updates on new releases, contests, and promotions, please go to AbsolutelyAmazingEbooks.com and sign up.

Bonus

If you will go to the Absolutely Amazing eBooks online bookstore (AbsolutelyAmazingEbooks.com) and enter the password below into the Bonus Reward Section, you can access recipes for many of the dishes you read about in this book – for free!

AA1061

ABOUT THE AUTHOR

Marjory Sorrell Rockwell says needlecraft arts – quilting, crocheting, knitting – are pastimes every woman can appreciate. And she particularly loves quiltmaking. "It's like painting with cloth," she says. But when not quilting she writes mysteries about a Midwestern sleuth not unlike herself, a middle-aged lady with an unpredictable family and loyal friends. And she's a big fan of watermelon pie.

ABSOLUTELY AMAZING eBOOKS

AbsolutelyAmazingeBooks.com
or AA-eBooks.com